W9-COP-122

FEARLESS LOVE

A BENNETT AFFAIR BOOK 1

DONNIA MARIE

Copyright © 2018 by Donnia Marie

FEARLESS LOVE

A BENNETT AFFAIR BOOK 1

All rights reserved.

This is a work of fiction. Names, characters, businesses, places, events, locales, and incidents are either the products of the author's imagination or used in a fictitious manner. Any resemblance to actual persons, living or dead, or actual events is purely coincidental.

No part of this book may be reproduced in any form or by any electronic or mechanical means, including information storage and retrieval systems, without written permission from the author, except for the use of brief quotations in a book review.

CAN'T GET ENOUGH?

Text **DONNIA** to **345345** to SUBSCRIBE to the
newsletter and stay on top of what's happening, events, book
releases and more!

FIND OUT MORE HERE

EMAIL: Info@DonniaMarie.com

For anyone second guessing love or have doubts about anything in life. Let go of the past, fears, and move forward...

CHAPTER ONE

CHELSEA

BRIGHT LIGHTS BEAMED EVERYWHERE. A camera was positioned to my left while the other peered straight ahead of me. Here we all sat at a humongous roundtable, in the dining room eating and talking. After a few lines here and there, my time came to speak.

"Uncle Dan, I'm tired of going back and forth with Nicole. I don't want to be here anymore. I'm sick of this family and all the hidden secrets you all keep. As a matter of fact, since you like to keep so many secrets, tell Nicole what really happened to Aunt Pam!"

After my statement, I paused and glared as it stated in my script. *"CUT!"* The director yelled. Finally, as midnight quickly approached, I finished my last scene.

My phone vibrated as I reached for it. There were six missed calls from Sean, ten from Shooter Ro and twelve from

Riana. What the hell could be that important? I thought to myself.

I decided to call Shooter first since I still helped manage his image in the rap game. "Damn, you in LA acting funny now. Let me find out you not being productive and leaving me and my career behind. You know I need someone with sense to help me."

"Shooter really? I've been taping. I told you things would be changing soon as your PR rep. And please, remember, I could never leave you hanging. But you know I have other things to focus on, so it's only so much I'll be able to do with your music. Hell, you so big in the game, there are thousands of people that would want to be your PR Representative."

After ending my statement, he took a deep breath. I could tell he hated the idea of losing me. I'd helped temporarily when he started rapping and he ended up using me long-term to represent him. I had a way of finding solutions for his stupid actions and turned them into something positive. Shooter's notorious reputation emphasized his gang affiliations in the past, so people knew not to mess with him.

What's interesting about Shooter is the fact that women still flocked to him regardless of his drama. We'd known each other since our early years and I can't deny how attractive he'd grown to be. His frame stood at about 5'11, slim build, shredded with muscles with tons of art decor on his arms and chest. Shooter had a likeness to Ray J and damn sure acted silly like him too. Unfortunately, the anger and temperament Shooter possessed turned me all the way off.

The night had just begun and the plan was to meet my

very good friend Sean B at 1 Oak Nightclub, off of West Hollywood. He just released an album and the energy around it buzzed worldwide. The popularity of his music set a trend for all other artists, and many in the industry consulted with him. He was unstoppable. Every track ended up number one. He'd been one of the hottest rappers for the past couple of years after ending a football career.

Of course, girls loved him, hell I couldn't even front dude is fine as hell. Sean stood around 6'5 and towered over my little self. I only measured 5'4. His six-pack added more value to the firm packed muscles he possessed on his arms. And his smile could brighten any darkness. He really favored Drake with the complexion and low haircut.

Many consider him the total package. He's handsome, runs multiple businesses on top of his music career, and he's a protector all topped off with street credibility. He isn't the type to look for trouble but if you brought it to him, he'd damn sure finish it.

I called a few times and no answer, so I decided to text.

Me: *Sean, sorry! I know I'm late but I'm not sure I will make it, I mean it's already midnight. Plus, I got a bad headache but enjoy your album release party. Make sure you party hard for both of us.*

Sean always had an entourage with him, so I'm sure he wouldn't miss me anyway.

I stepped outside, waiting on my driver to take me back to my hotel. Before I knew it, my best friend Riana called again.

"Chelsea, why your background so quiet? I thought I

would hear all the music and commotion of the album release party? I mean, you not gon go support your boy?" Riana stays fishing for answers, she thinks Sean and I like each other but my response stays the same, there is no interest on either end.

"I want too, but we just wrapped up on set and I feel like my head is 'bout to explode. I have been feeling this pressure around my head lately. Maybe it's because I'm here in LA. Back home in Atlanta, I was fine." Riana remained quiet for a second then went on and on about how messed up that would be, since Sean is usually supportive of my successes.

Changing the subject, I asked about her life and upcoming tour. Riana is a major singer, dancer, and actress. She's known as a triple threat. Riana's twenty-five years old, about a year younger than me. Not only did she have talent but she was stunningly beautiful. She stood about 5'7, very light skinned, favoring Alicia Keys a bit and she loved to wear her long, curly, hair out and wild. We met at school when we were about thirteen. Joy always filled me to call her my best friend. She always had my back and I always had hers.

"Hey Nick, take me to 1 Oak please." I voiced to my driver as we pulled off. Riana made me feel so bad that I decided to just go to the party. I'd packed some extra clothes before filming since my plans were to go in the first place, so I was covered with appropriate club attire.

On my way to the club, I burst out laughing. I reminisced about getting caught by the director changing my clothes in the bathroom moments before Nick arrived to get me.

"YEAH! You the shit with yo fine ass," I hollered,

twerking and rolling my ass in the mirror. I wore a sleeveless, white Dior dress that showed every curve I had in my body.

I went braless since the dress wasn't meant to be rocked with one and I added a jean jacket to my waist, in hopes it would appear more casual. My feet consisted of a pair of Fendi boots that wrapped around my leg, stopping a little bit over my ankle. To finish the look, I added my gold Fendi Watch.

Looking into the mirror, I seemed flawless and the hair-stylist who did my hair rocked the crap out of my strands. I had a nice side part; My hair straight and flowing beautifully to the midsection of my back. I could only hope the humidity and dancing wouldn't send my natural hair into a huge puff.

The line outside was still long and it was a little after one am. 1 Oak was thick, and I could only imagine what the inside held. "Chelsea, oh wow, it's great to see you supporting your friend Sean. You are here for him, right?" I looked at her with a slight smile and kept walking. These paparazzi people were a trip.

The speakers blasted Drake's song, 🎵 'Mob Ties' as I walked in. I quickly tried to make my way to VIP where I saw Sean's security and his whole entourage.

The club was beautifully decorated as the chandelier lights shined throughout the club, illuminating the space giving it a scenic look. The ambiance in the club was a whole vibe and the partygoers added to it by being all the way turnt.

The crowds were starting to notice me, and I saw people with their phones out trying to snap. I didn't care to make a scene, I always been quite shy in a sense, but people would never know it.

Finally, I made it near VIP and security escorted me up. Sean didn't know of my arrival, and I was glad because I wanted to surprise him.

The VIP section had the plushest seating areas I'd ever seen. The caramel leather seats sat high and the vaulted ceilings were amazing. This area had a different type of lighting that set a tone of sophistication.

Champagne juices flew everywhere. The bottle girls weren't playing that night, they wore white shorts that showed 80% of their butt cheeks and the bra like shirts were see through. Nonetheless, all the girls were beautiful, and they made sure the VIP section was secure.

The man I sought out stood in plain sight. I saw Sean with his homeboy Dion, over the gold rail talking and looking down at the crowd, bobbing their heads. Sean's style was a whole mood. I noticed his big gold SB chain around his neck, glistening so damn bright, with diamond cuts running all through it. He rocked some white pants with a fitted green and yellow Gucci shirt and some all black Yeezys. Seeing his muscle physique through the shirt put the icing on the cake. He outdid the mess out of his fit.

I crept up, wrapping my arms around him, while still trying to conceal my identity. I rapped the lyrics that were now blasting. Obviously, he heard and noticed my voice over the loud music and crowd. Without looking back, he brushed his hands over my arms then placed his hands on top of mine.

"So you made it after all?" I could see his smile despite him facing the crowd. As quick as he said that, he turned to face me and hugged me. I set my face right above his stomach, inhaling the mesmerizing whiff of his cologne. The smell of him alone would drive anyone crazy. We were both happy to see each other and we started turnin' up to the music.

We were face to face rapping, singing, dancing and the night continued with the rest of the VIP guests. Then his new hit song came on and the club went off the wall. Sean was amped, the song only been out for 24 hours but yet the club goers knew it. So, I got in his face and started rapping his own lyrics to him.

♪♪ *"I got the drip and these fuck niggas mad*
Baggin they bitches while I turn up my swag
Pulling up in my new Lambo Veneno
$10.5 Million, what the fuck does he know?"

Before I could finish rapping and vibing, he joined me, and the crowd hailed.

"Yass fuck it up, sis!"
"Are y'all together?"
"Oh my God, Sean!"
"We love you, Chelsea!"
"You better bag her bruh."

I got real big headed. From the looks of it, we were a hit! Just like that my headache was gone or at least I forgot about it. About an hour in, I knew I needed to go. I had to be back on set at eight am. I congratulated Sean and we exchanged a few words but then he followed me out. We went through a secret exit so the fans wouldn't notice him.

Walking out the back door, I observed how clear the sky appeared and the stars beamed brightly at us. The cool night's air made me feel good. More importantly, I managed to come out and support Sean. Once outside, Sean wrapped his arms around my neck and started talking, "When did you learn the lyrics to my song? Cause in the studio, you act like you weren't listening."

I laughed. That day was crazy in the studio, but I didn't miss a beat. "Of course, I listened. I'm your friend and one of your biggest supporters, Sean." He seemed happy to hear that, but only replied with his eyes and licking his lips, while nodding slowly.

"Well, I'm a fan of yours too, you know. So how was your first day of filming? I mean, it's a new show for you and you are a series regular now, which means you will be working a lot with this cast. Are you still up for it? This *is* what you wanted!"

Looking up at him I smiled, "Yeah, it was great but long. I met so many cool people, and I had a few fans too, which made me feel good. I'm just not sure I'm ready to make that big move here from Atlanta."

He gave me a puzzled look. "What you mean, I thought that's what you wanted? Is it the finances, fear or...?"

"No, my finances are fine. I just don't want to leave Camden."

"Oh ok, I understand. Well, you know I got you if needed. I will always have your back, Chelsea." I could see the concern in Sean's face but I also knew he meant every word.

We were quiet for a while, which led me to think how great of a friend and support we had been to each other. We met six years prior and been good friends ever since. Honestly, Sean was someone I talked to about everything. He knew who I been talking too and things that I wouldn't share with the average person. I even knew who he smashed and the crazy things he would go out and do. Our bond was unbreakable.

CHAPTER TWO

SEAN

A COOL BREEZE hit my face while wrapping my arms around Chelsea. I loved hearing about her progress in life. She's a hard worker that's ambitious as hell and she had become a very good friend of mine.

Despite how fine she was, I knew I couldn't ever take it there. I watched her, admiring how beautiful she was as her form-fitting dress hugged her physique. Her slim waist was very visible and her sun-kissed skin from her legs and face radiated underneath the stars. She may be short but every feature on her body compliments her well.

Then my mind went back to hearing her rap my lyrics in the club, which made me feel something extra for her and the thought made my dick throb. I was glad, I knew then she either been bumping my music non-stop or she really had been in tune when I recorded that night in the studio. In reality, her magnetic energy intrigued me and I felt so much support from her. I could only imagine what the blogs would have up in the morning.

Peering down with a smile, I watched her picture-perfect full lips. The way she exaggerated with her thin eyebrows while trying to prove a point always made me laugh. Lost in my thoughts, I didn't even notice her getting quiet. In a whisper, she asked, "Sean what the hell is wrong with you, why are you staring at me in a daze?"

I gawked down at her for a second and brushed the tip of my fingers on her small pointy nose, "Nothing, just thinking about life and how blessed we are." Of course, I lied, not wanting to tell her how fond I'd been of her at the moment.

She pushed me back and laughed not buying my lie. All of a sudden, we could hear the crickets. We were silent, which was rare because we never had a dry moment. Our conversations were always live, but tonight not so much. I gently pushed her back, "So when the next time we're getting up with each other? It's been a while since we sat down for dinner to catch up." Chelsea and I chatted on the phone at least once a week and we would meet up in person anytime we were in the same area.

She let out a long sigh, "I don't even know... My schedule is so busy that I can't even wrap my mind around anything. But how can you ask me that when you're the one that's about to be on tour for like six months? Not to mention all the deals you have going on. I'm sure we won't be talking much anyway." Damn, she sounded concerned. I smiled, realizing I felt the same way about her too. I had been calling her, but our talks were so brief due to the increase of roles she received, but I was happy for her. That didn't change the fact that I did miss confiding in her.

"That's why I'm asking you now about us finding time while you here in LA!"

After hearing me get smart and avoiding my statement, she looked back up at me and moved in closer, holding my hands with our fingers linked. "Sean you are so good to me you know that? Every time I need someone to listen to me rant you're there. Even when you don't answer, you always find a way to reply back and I appreciate that."

"So, what are you saying Chelsea?" She leaned in and rested her head on my chest. We had to be standing there just breathing each other in for a solid five minutes.

I knew then why it seemed different. Our emotions had caught up to us and our bond had grown exponentially. But I knew she wouldn't want to go further than that.

"Oh my god, standing here with you, I forgot to let Nick know to pick me up... Ugh," Chelsea shouted and pulled out her phone.

My nose flared, "Who's Nick?"

"Oh, I forgot we haven't talked much lately. Yeah, that's part of my package deal. My agent negotiated for the production to pay for my room, travel fees, and a few miscellaneous things. I chose a driver as part of it. I really hate driving in LA traffic."

I understood that, but I didn't want her riding late with no man, driver or not. "How about I get my driver to take you back to your hotel and I can ride if you want me too?"

"No, Sean I'll be fine; Besides you need to go back inside,

the party will be ending soon an—" before she could finish her statement...

"Yeah, Sean, everyone's been looking for you. Why you out here hiding?" Lexi yelled while coming out the back door of the club and observing Chelsea. "Oh, hey Chelsea. You came out to the club to get you a man, huh? I can tell by your outfit you're looking for one."

Chelsea seemed unbothered but ranted back, "Girl please, you know damn well men flock to me regardless. I ain't nothing like you, besides, you the one that's been with everybody in the industry, right?"

Lexi being an amazing artist would be an understatement because she holds many accolades in her field. But she also has a reputation that follows her for being an industry hoe. I didn't invite her to my album release party but somehow, she showed up. Surprisingly many came through. Rappers, singers, actors and all types were in attendance. But my only concern at the moment was making sure Chelsea got back to her hotel safely.

Chelsea hadn't moved away from me since Lexi came out. Chelsea stood in front of me but against me. Her back touching my abs and her butt touching my groin area. I don't think she noticed since she stood listening to Lexi shout. Chelsea knew I had sex with Lexi before and of course, Lexi never cared for me and Chelsea's friendship either. Shoot, even the media would throw rumors around about us dating, and though I wish they were true, it wasn't.

"Lexi why you out here checking for me? I didn't even invite you." She looked hurt as she dropped her head down sobbing with tears. "Fuck you, Sean! It's easy for you to say when you don't give a fuck about no one else's feelings." She stormed back in leaving Chelsea and I standing there.

I noticed Chelsea hitting the send button for her driver, so I knew there was no point of stopping her now. As the all black Denali pulled up, Chelsea turned back around to face me. "Sean, I'm so fucking happy for you right now. I guess those sleepless hours you put in is paying off. You really inspire me and I hope we can always be there for one another."

"Ssshh," I whispered, placing one finger to her lips, pulling her closer to me. The aroma she possessed held me captive. I was losing it.

Glaring down, biting my bottom lip, I stroked her shoulders eventually making it down her back until it landed on her waist. We mounted like statues as I took in her hypnotic eyes. She twitched, while her hands laid still on the back of my arms. Her fingers danced in slow motion over my skin. I could sense her breathing pattern changing as she started moving her legs together in a way that made me think she was hot and bothered in between her legs. I was turned on than a motherfucka and I was sure she could feel my erectness touching her belly.

I leaned down placing a kiss on her forehead. She gripped me tighter, so I went to kiss her lips but she pulled away. "Unh unh Sean," she pouted. It was at that moment I knew I was out of control. I fucking wanted her but didn't want to fuck shit up.

"Sean, I gotta go. I'll text you when I make it back to the

room." I nodded and walked her to the door, opening it for her, "Goodnight Chelsea."

"Goodnight Sean."

I watched the car drive off until it disappeared.

The music grew louder and louder as I got closer to the main area.

"There goes Sean!"

"Sean!"

"Sean B," the crowd went wild. But I was still stuck on the fact I tried to kiss Chelsea and she curved me. I wasn't sweating it though. I knew I needed to stay focused and not fuck our friendship up anyways.

"Damn nigga, fuck you been?" Benji shouted in my ear.

"Nowhere, I just walked Chelsea to the car."

Benji looked at me with a raised brow, "That's what's up man, it's good to see you guys going strong. But why don't you two make it official? Y'all hang out at each other's spots and go out to dinner. Hell, y'all seem to be together to me."

I knew my little brother was right. But what did this 23-year-old know? He's the same one fucking everything that had a pussy. Girls would give their whole soul away, I laughed at the thought. I guess since he played for the Los Angeles Snakes as a quarterback and usually was crowned MVP, he was a golddigger's target. He was the star of the team and they had been undefeated for the past two Super Bowls.

The music slowed down as the DJ shouted me out, "Let's give it up for Sean B. His album is off the charts right now. He is number one on iTunes, Spotify, and all other streaming services. He is doing it big— and Sean B, as you can see we all fuck with you. We love you, man."

The crowd roared and I felt good as hell. Me being me, I started making it rain, hundreds falling everywhere. What the hell I do that for? The women and men went bonkers. Then the DJ started spinning my tracks and the crowd sang along. I was amped as Benji igged me on to take a few shots. We threw them back to back causing my throat to burn but that didn't bother me since life seemed to be flowing smoothly.

"Damn he fine."

"I'll fuck the shit out of you Sean."

"We love you, Sean."

I heard it all that night. I was feeling so good that I took my Gucci shirt off and threw it into the crowd. That caused a big commotion, and within seconds a brawl broke out between some girls below me.

Damn, I didn't expect that. I was just trying to show some love. After things simmered down I went to one of the private rooms to settle down. The room began to spin so I took time out to just breathe.

I fell against the tan leather couch, in return it pushed me back up. I looked down and noticed sweat beads plaguing my body causing my abs to glisten. Damn, I was ripped and at that very moment, I could understand why the girls were trippin on the sight of my shirt coming off.

I was glad I could finally reap the benefits of my hard work. I was drafted to play in the NFL for the Patriots before I received my degree, much to my parent's detriment. My talent on the field spoke for itself, but I got a career-ending injury early in my football career. I was upset about it, but not completely heartbroken. Although I loved football, music was my passion. So I took that passion and established a music career and have been soaring ever since. My musicality has gotten better over the years and with the help of a great team, I am building an empire.

Now I can smile at all my accomplishments and all the investments I had under my belt. My parents taught me and my brothers well. It was three of us and we all had great careers going. I was the rapper with a lot of business ventures, Benji was a star quarterback player, and my older brother Sebastien was a lawyer who part owned a basketball team.

"Sean, I want you." Instantly I was knocked out my daze as I felt hands on my abs. Opening my eyes I saw a blurry face but I knew it had to be Lexi. Seconds later, her hands made its way to my belt.

"Lexi, look you cool and all but I ain't trying to have sex with you. I just want to sober up and go home."

"Well, let me take you home then and we can finish there." As quick as she said that I was sober enough to make my next move. A move that she wasn't happy with.

I stood up and told her to leave. She was pissed as hell. Pointing her fingers and fussing she yelled, "I knew you were fucking that bitch. Fucking liar. You so damn stupid!" As if those words weren't enough, she came up and mushed my head and that had me angry. I turned back around and got in her face and started yelling enough to scare her.

"I should beat your mothafuckin ass, but I'm better than that. But if you keep fucking around, I'll get the right one to lay yo ass out!" I could see the fear in her eyes as she trembled but then she opened her mouth to speak. I let her ramble on and walked off. I didn't have time to put up with a girl that I didn't want, let alone, one that I had no obligation to.

I felt bad initially, I didn't believe in disrespecting any woman, PERIOD! But she was a nuisance to me and I could tell if I wasn't firm, she wouldn't let up.

Pulling my phone out, I noticed Chelsea's name on the screen and instantly my heart raced. I made my way to the private bathroom across from me so I could answer her call, "I'm glad you made it home."

"Yeah, I'm in the bed settled in. I called because I thought you might have made it in." I looked at the time and already it read four am. The club remained in full throttle but I knew it was time to leave.

"Nah, I'm kind of fucked up but I'm gonna call my driver now. I'll call you when I get home if you want?" Damn, I was feeling weak for this girl and I couldn't understand why now.

"You can if you want, I might be sleeping since I have to be up in three hours but at least text me to let me know that you made it home." My dick soared at every word she released. She wasn't even doing anything and I was feeling reckless.

"Damn in three hours? Yeah, get you some rest and I'll

text you when I get in. But in case I don't get to talk to you, I wanna wish you luck on your second day on set."

"Thanks, Sean, I lo— will talk to you later." She quickly hung up. Damn was she about to tell me she loved me. I wanted to question her but I didn't. I decided to let it go.

"Benji I'm about to go home. You good?" Benji was in another private room and I should have known better than to ask that. He sat there getting head by some Hispanic chick. "Yeah man, I'll holla at ya." I shook my head and left.

CHAPTER THREE

CHELSEA

I WATCHED the numbers light up in the elevator as we sailed up. After two weeks of being in LA, I finally made it back to Atlanta and was ready to relax with Cam. I gazed out at the open floor plan of my condo and exhaled. I resided on the 22nd floor and had an amazing panoramic view of the Midtown Atlanta skyline. I'm gonna miss this, I thought to myself. I only had a few more weeks before I moved to LA.

"Mom, do you think we're gonna like Los Angeles? Is our new apartment going to look like this?"

"Cam, I think we will both love LA. You're just going to finish the school term out with grandma and grandpa at their house then you will be with me, in LA." Cam looked up and smiled. He loved my parents and the great thing about living in my place was they lived down the street.

"What about daddy?" I looked down at him and smirked, "Of course you will still see your daddy."

Cam had a very close relationship with his dad since he was active in his life from the beginning. Randall had been my high school sweetheart and during our senior year I ended up pregnant. Lucky for me, my parents helped with Camden while we managed to go off to college with no issues. After college, he was drafted into the NBA, joining the Atlanta team. Everything seemed great until I heard that he was not only cheating, but he'd gotten someone else pregnant. Of course I confronted him despite being hurt and feeling violated.

He admitted to it and I broke up with him immediately. Once the baby was born, he took a DNA test, which confirmed he wasn't the father. We were both happy but my trust for him was gone and a relationship between us would no longer work.

No one ever knew about the drama at the time except us, but I couldn't let go of the fact that he cheated. Now that Camden's eight, I've learned to forgive Randall but we would never be involved again.

When it came to taking care of family, Randall would be considered selfless. Financially, he provided monthly for the both of us and though I told him I didn't need anything for myself, he still gave an extra $3,000 on top of what he gave Cam. With my acting career and my job as a PR Rep, my bank account wasn't hurting.

"Man, y'all ain't got no food up in here?" Randall rambled while opening my refrigerator. I came out of the room and looked at him like he was crazy. "What? You left the front door cracked and I walked in." He paused and started again, "And where my boy Camden at? He ain't called me all week and that's not normal for him."

"He's asleep now, he usually takes a nap after school."

Randall was still fine and the money he made enhanced every area in his life. Our senior year, his height stood at 6'2 but by the time he was drafted that dude had made it to 6'7. He was built like hell with tattoos all over his chest and arms. He even had a beautiful picture of Cam on his left arm.

His rich dark skin shined anytime and any day. He used to wear man buns all the time but this particular day I noticed he cut it off and got them waves popping, which caused his facial hair to appear thicker. Cam looked just like him, just a smaller and younger version.

I watched him move from the stainless-steel fridge over to my marble countertop that took up half of my kitchen. He observed my decor like this was his first time in there. He touched my white and grey leather sectional that seats ten. Next, he sat down looking at my dangling silver lights. When you're sitting in my living room you can look behind you and find the all-white dining set and to the left, my kitchen sits looking flawless. Since we're barely at home, things stayed pretty neat.

The sun beaming on Randall caused me to notice his earrings and necklace. I even observed the ring on his finger from basketball. "What's your plan while in LA? What can I do to help you and Cam? Since he is staying with your parents, I figured I would get him more and possibly hire a nanny or something."

I listened to him but thought differently, "Nah, I think my

parents will do just fine and whenever you're available you can get him and do whatever you want."

He agreed but asked me to come on the balcony with him to talk. I didn't see why we needed to go outside, but I followed him anyways across the living room. He slid the balcony door open and shut the door behind me. I viewed the big, tall, shiny windows of the Georgia Power building across from me. I looked down at the cars passing and the people on the other side walking.

"I know you heard about me possibly getting a contract in LA." I looked at him stupidly. I heard about it but never mentioned it since he never told me personally. As I stood there silently, he grabbed me aggressively but with some sense of love.

"You are so beautiful to me Chels!—And I was thinking if I sign that contract and move to LA that maybe we can try dating again and see where things go." I busted out laughing and he wasn't happy. He raised both brows and frowned.

"Dude are you serious? Nope! Nope-nope-nope-never-gonna-happen. Never in my life will I be that dumb. Did you just forget about the scandal between you and Tracey? I can go on and on."

Tracey is the daughter of a congressman and it was reported that she and Randall had been dating but things escalated when she found out he messed with another girl who happened to be the daughter of a local reporter. The situation got worse because both girls ended up fighting over him. Just plain stupid and ugly to outsiders looking in.

"Chels I get it but I never loved these other women and I

always kept it real from the start with all of them. It was fun and games but now I want something stable. Chels, we know each other so well and the history we have no one can compare to that."

I left Randall on the balcony, talking to himself and sat on my couch. He followed shortly. My focus followed the people on Love & Hip Hop until he sat down next to me. He was so close I could damn near hear his heartbeat. Unfortunately, the attraction between us still seemed to be there, but I knew he wasn't shit so I didn't entertain it.

"Daddy!" Camden jumped in his lap and started talking about everything. I decided to let them connect and walked out.

I picked up the phone, Sean: **Damn Chelsea, where you been at? I haven't heard a word from you. You aight?**

My heart fluttered at the sight of Sean's name in my messages. I forgot to get back to him.

Me: **Sorry I been so busy, what the hell you up too?**

We went back and forth until Randall startled me.

"Who got you smiling so hard?" Before opening my mouth... "Oh, your so-called best friend I see. So, what's up, are you fucking him?" I shook my head no.

Randall rubbed his fingers through his thick long beard, viewing my gestures to see if I was truthful. Damn, he turned me on and I could feel myself getting wet. I hated the fact that Randall still appealed to me. But I rejected the thoughts and advanced to the corner where my desk and laptop were, to study my lines.

Time flew by, my room no longer had any sunlight. I didn't notice how late it got. I showered and got in the bed and finally, I heard Randall leaving and shouting he was gone. Cam slid in my bed and fell fast asleep.

A text flashed on my phone, Randall: ***I made sure Cam showered and he ate. We also did homework together for the week. So get you some rest Chels. And just in case I don't tell you enough, I appreciate you for all you do with Camden. I do notice and I love you like hell for that. Thank you!*** 😘

The week had come for me to start packing for LA. I hadn't done anything because I was too busy managing Shooter. This fucker got in a fight with a man and threatened his life while cameras were everywhere. To make matters worse, he showed his ass in court. It took me a while to try to find a game plan for his image in the media, plus the lawyers only allowed certain things to be spoken about the event via the public. Quite frankly, after all the drama I was actually glad I would only be focusing on myself and my career.

I was exhausted and fell stomach first hitting my Tempurpedic bed. I had finally packed up the bulk of my things that I would send to LA. "Damn Sean, so that's how you answer my FaceTime calls now?" I stared at a topless Sean with water droplets sliding down his face and chest. I sneered at the look of him licking and biting his bottom lips. Damn, damn, damn he was fine and I had the nerve to consider him a best friend of mine.

"Chelsea, I ain't fucking witcha no more. You never hit me up. We always been so close and talk about everything but you been acting different lately." His eyes were piercing through the screen with seriousness.

Talking to him brought me so much joy that I didn't even remember walking towards my balcony. I was on a natural high and didn't know how I would make it back down.

"Sean, really? What's up? Let's catch up."

"Yeah let's talk. Why you ain't tell me you fucking with Dorien now? It took the blogs and media outlets for me to find out."

"What? No, I'm not. We went out a few times but we not fucking. Besides, he's the lead in the show and we really vibe but that's it. You should know me better than that. I always tell you things, Sean." I smirked at Sean, he hesitated but smiled back, he knew I wouldn't lie to him about fucking anyone.

Shoot, I would come to his house sometimes after some of my dates with others. There were even times when I knew he had sex with whoever and later that night me and Sean would Netflix and chill at his place. We were just cool as hell. But lately, I could feel the change between us and I knew we were feeling more for each other than we wanted too.

"You talk all that shit and I listen to you about your hoes, but aren't you supposed to be Daddy Long Stroke? That's what you said them hoes call you right?" He snapped his head back giggling. Those were the stories he told me when he was messing with different celebrity chicks. I mean we talked about everything.

"I am feeling him though." Sean's face dropped at the mere thought of me having an attraction to Dorien. He listened to me go on and on. "Sean, you never cared when I told you about other guys, we always joke about it, just like when you tell me about Lexi and her head game or the three-somes in the past. Plus, you know how my trust is with men in the industry. I don't think I can be with anyone that's in the spotlight."

I paused. He wasn't looking at me anymore. His focus remained only on himself. I watched his lengthy arms mois-turize his muscular legs as the towel wrapped around his waist lifted. The thick print that bulged from the towel had me fantasizing on what I could do to him. I caught myself panting quietly but got focused when I felt my bud thumping.

"I don't mind hearing anything you have to say, actually I want you to find someone that makes you happy. I was just confused when they said it was confirmed that you two were together and you were officially off the market. Usually, you be so geeked about whatever news and hit me up. *Shiiiit*, don't let me not answer your call or return the call fast enough then you quick to text me, dm me and anything else because of your excitement."

We both chuckled. I knew he was right. Any news mean-ingful to me would make its way to him because I made sure to relay the message voluntarily or involuntarily.

Enthusiastically, I yelled, "That's why I fuck with you, Sean. I love how open we are with each other."

I toned it down with a warm whisper, "But I do miss you though and I hope we can see each other soon. I don't want you to go on tour before seeing me. Can we make that happen?"

"Maybe, Chelsea, just maybe."

A knock on my door startled me out my sleep. It's Saturday and I wasn't expecting anyone. Swinging the door open I saw a bunch of neatly packaged gifts sitting on the floor. "Who the hell would just leave something like this at my front door?"

I carried all three boxes in and finally found the card.

Chelsea,

"If you ever doubt how much I love you!"

My heart protruded out my chest, the thought of someone doing this made me anxious.

I unraveled the first small box and it read...

Cartier: DIAMANTS LÉGERS EARRINGS, MM (Yellow Gold Diamonds). The circular stud earrings were beautiful. But the diamonds inside were PRICELESS.

Panic ran through me. Who the hell would send me such expensive gifts and I'm single as hell? Not to mention how stingy I am with my yoni. I haven't had sex in about year.

Box   2:   **PANTHÈRE   DE   CARTIER**

SUNGLASSES, whoever was sending these knew I had a thing for jewelry and sunglasses.

Box 3: **PANTHÈRE DE CARTIER WATCH**.

I was grateful but uneasy. I loved gifts but hated to let people spend money on me. I felt I could get what I wanted for myself. That's another reason why I put all the extra money Randall gives me in Camden's savings account. It bothered me to hear stories about the mothers who would make wealthy fathers pay crazy amounts for child support. I see it like this, if the dad is in the kid's life and provides financially and they aren't stingy, then let them be.

I walked around the house in awe of my gifts but was still very curious about the mysterious sender. I wanted to call Randall but I didn't. Honestly, I wanted to call anybody that I knew expressed their love for me but decided to stay quiet.

"Riana, ok, so I need you to shut up and listen!" —— There was a long pause.

"*Hellooo,* did you hear me Ria?"

"Duh I heard you, Chelsea, you said to shut up and listen, so I'm listening!"

"Oh, yeah my bad, you know I need to at least hear you breathing or something. —— So, I got a package today and it's Cartier everything. Cartier Earrings, Cartier Sunglasses, and a Cartier Gold Watch..."

Riana gasped for air, "*Really!* What? Who running they check on you like this and you not fucking no one, nothing, nada, nada da-yuuum thang?"

"Shut up Ria but yea, I'm confused. But I'mma find out."

"Maybe it's your baby daddy Randall. He does have a

new basketball contract in LA or maybe it's Sean. He can afford it since he's the only few people in the world with a Lambo Veneno. — Hey, I meant to ask you what the hell was he thinking to spend so much money on a damn car? Even me being who I am with my celebrity status and financial circumstances, I don't think I would spend that much. But I'll continue to sip my tea and watch you two perform like Beyoncé and Jay on TV."

"Girl shut up, I was just supporting him at the album release party. I'm so sick of those media outlets and blogs talking shit that they know nothing about."

"Get over the media, it's just the beginning for you, especially with your acting career. But girl I gotta get back to the makeup room, I'm due to perform in forty-five minutes. I will call you later."

"K, love you Ria and show the fuck out!"

"Love you too Chels and *biiitch*, you know I will!"

CHAPTER FOUR

SEAN

I'D JUST TOUCHED down in Atlanta a few hours back and decided to enjoy some downtime before hitting the streets. I stayed at the W in Downtown since its closest to Chelsea. Besides, being here allowed me to link up with family. I've always been big about family and never wanted to go long without physically seeing them. Especially my older brother Sebastien. He's always on the go, but he too stayed put in Atlanta to attend our parent's get together. We were having a big family cookout the day before I return to LA.

My free time in the hotel consisted of working out and going for a swim. It felt perfect to relax and be alone for a change. That is until my momma popped up.

"Hey, baby! Look at you. You look so healthy and *handsome* of course." My mom shouted as I opened the door entering my suite. She flaunted a dressy black bodysuit. She added one of those long sweaters that fell like a dress. My mom didn't look forty-nine at all. She was very youthful looking and her medium build complimented her 5'5 height perfectly.

We talked and laughed as she asked about the details that were mentioned in the blogs about Dorien and Chelsea. She questioned what I wanted with her as well. My mom knew and loved Chelsea, but knew the reasons behind Chelsea's trust issues.

"Momma, I don't even know. I know I love her and all but she's worried about being cheated on and what people will think if she's with someone who makes money since her baby daddy is a ballplayer and all these other things. I know for a fact she not trying to be with Dorien because he's like me."

"Like you, as in having females flock to you and having money?"

I put my head down with shame and nodded.

"Well, she does have every reason to be worried, who wouldn't be? You know what? I want you to focus on your career, but if you know she's worth it and you say you love her then move on from friends and try a relationship."

Pleading for help I continued to pour out my feelings, "Mom, I can't even stop thinking about her. Day in day out, she's what I think of first and last. It never used to be like this. I don't know what happened, but I fell hard. And what's worse is the fact that it hurts me to even think she would date anyone other than me.... I am in love with her." That was the first time I admitted that out loud.

My mom's mouth dropped open with a slight, knowing smirk.

"Well son, I think you know what to do. One thing for sure, I know Chelsea and she is one hell of a mother. And she's humble. Do you see how much she gives her time to help people she doesn't know?"

Her statement brought me back to the time Chelsea and I was in New York for a charity event. We'd spent a whole day donating clothes and shoes for children going back to school. It was her idea to start with, but I knew her passion and I wanted to help. Collectively, we'd given thousands of dollars, and later, several people chipped in to give more. As if that wasn't enough, she decided to sponsor a family for a whole year on her own. Seeing her give like that showed me her heart wasn't all on money and I could only pray to find a woman with a pure soul as hers.

After our trip from New York, I would leave money at her house to compensate for all she poured out into the charity. Chelsea being her always returned the money, no matter how much I refused to take it back. It was to a point she would hide the money in my house somewhere and a week later tell me to check whichever spot. As she would put it, "Sean, I give because I care. I'm in a good position to help so I refuse to let kids suffer. That could have been me."

I pulled out of my daze and continued listening to my mom.

"Oh, and she's wise with money and that's something you need to get on board with too. You spend entirely too much."

"You right, I do need to wife her."

"Hoooooooold-up-now, I like that idea but take it slow."

With laughter, my hands raised in defense but I knew what she meant.

After our talk, I took my mom out for lunch and sent her off for a spa day. I always went all out for her and my dad, but he was out on a mission trip for the church. So, I needed to make sure my mom remained her best until he got back.

Our talk made me realize I needed to figure out what I wanted and move forward. Chelsea was indecisive, but as a man, I knew I should take the lead. The only issue was my mind was in a cluster fuck of its own. Being single worked for me because I could go as I please. But then the thought of monogamy plagued me because women who I knew fucked niggas while still laying up with their main man. I didn't want to be one of them.

The spotlight always put a focus on you and makes you question who's really with you. So many girls just wanted the money and fame. My little brother Benji was a prime example of that. He had chicks coming at him left and right and he never trusted their motives. After one too many proved it was about the money and his status, he never treated relationships with females as more than bedroom time.

Thoughts of Chelsea using me never crossed my mind. She made her own money and maintained her own savings account. I've never seen her go after men for money, ever. She always seemed thoughtful of me too. Just a few weeks prior, we got tested for STD's, which Benji thought was funny. I did too because we weren't fucking each other but she said she knew I would never go on my own, which wasn't true because I got checked yearly.

I didn't argue with her, we got tested and a week later we viewed each other's results. The thought of it made me think she might want this dick after all. Who would go through all of that? But at least we knew each other's status.

I never got back to Chelsea about the tour but I'm sure she knew I had started. The tour remained a hot topic, it sold out in most venues, which in my book was a good thing. The day I talked to her was the day before it began. What I didn't tell her was I had two free days and after she'd ask me to make a way, I figured I'd swing by her place in Atlanta before she left for LA.

"Riana, what's good?"

"Nothing Sean... What's up?"

"I called to see if there's a way to find out Chelsea's schedule. I wanna holla at her but I kinda wanna surprise her."

There was a long pause but then...

"I'm *sooo* sick n tired of y'all, you know dat? — I had to talk to her for about three hours the other night about you and her feelings. I don't know what games y'all playin but y'all need a fix it ASAP! — I'm also concerned. As you already know she hasn't had sex in a year and I'm sure she's growing hella cobwebs down there, so beware! And FYI, if you don't hurry and make it official with her, Dorien or Randall will. Because both of em' want her. Thank me later!"

I died of laughter while checking the phone to see who I was really talking too. Riana is always straight up, but damn, I ain't asked her all of that either. However, she now had me thinking and she had all my attention. Eventually, she sent over the details on when Chelsea would be home.

Strolling down the hallway I recognized a voice. "I hope LA treats you as good as Atlanta has. Oh, and keep them niggas off you girl." I knew that was Randall's voice, and it was clear he was leaving Chelsea's place. It never bothered me on how they co-parent, as a matter of fact, none of her friendships or relationships bothered me since we were just friends but I couldn't control feeling a little jealous now.

"What's up Sean? I ain't seen you in a while, besides on TV." Randall was all smiles but his tone seemed suspicious.

"What up Randall? I heard about the contract deal for LA, congratulations."

I must have boosted his ego because the next three minutes was all about him, but shit I wasn't here for all of that so I cut him short.

"Well damn Sean, you must really be trying to get up with Chelsea, you all rushing and shit?"

"Something like that, I'm tryna catch up with her since she always on the move, plus I'm touring and thought I could chill wit' her. — Unless you got a problem you need to address with me?" I was getting impatient with dude and was ready to tell him about himself. But he didn't go further and went on about his business.

"Why the fuck you still here, what do you want Randall?" Chelsea fussed while opening the door but not looking to see that it was actually me.

Chelsea walked toward the couch, with her eyes glued to the TV. But my eyes were stuck on her sexy ass. She had on some black gym shorts that showed the tip of her ass cheeks, with a red crop top shirt. Her golden-brown natural hair was up in a bun and complimented her well.

She must've seen my reflection on the TV because she screamed, "Oh my God!" She turned jumping into my arms. We were face to face, my hands gripping her ass in order to keep her up. She straddled me wrapping her hands around my neck.

She hugged me so tight, dropping several kisses to either side of my cheeks. "Why yo big head ain't tell me you were coming over Sean? I would've made plans for us." I still had her in position, walking her to the counter to sit her on top of it.

"Well, why you ain't tell me you were still fucking Randall?" I gestured to her outfit.

"Whaaaateva, I don't want that boy." Chelsea grinned while spreading her legs open, giving me a slight view of her flesh below. "But if you want *"best friend"* you can smell and see how truthful I am."

My brows raised as I let out a chuckle, "Stop playing, you don't wanna go there." I joked slapping the inner part of her thigh.

My heart raced at the mere thought of touching her. But my dick.... Buddy had a mind of his own.

Placing her hands over mine, she responded, "But for real, he came by to get Cam's bag since he's getting him from my parent's house. Besides, you know I wear what I want and Randall couldn't get this if his life depended on it. I actually told him that the other day because he was talking nonsense about us getting back together."

"Mmhmm..." Brushing my tongue over my teeth, I tilted her chin up so our mouths could meet. At this point, I was gon give her all of me and she could either take it or leave it.

I fixed my lips on top of hers. Our tongues connected, moving to a rhythm that set my dick on fire. Everything in me desired to pull her apart but I took it slow. Moving my palms up and down her back, I gently gripped her flanks causing my elongated stick to press towards her opening. Pulling her head away, "Sean, what does this mean for us? I'm scared to take it there because I know our relationship will change."

Ignoring her, I drew her face towards me and kissed her passionately. With my mouth still on hers, "I'm in love with you Chelsea." Her hands moved from my face, stopping at my neck. She wrapped her legs around me tighter than before, trying to feel me in. "I love you too, Sean." Instantly a combustion happened inside of me and there was no stopping it.

I snatched her off the counter carrying her into the bedroom. She pulled her shirt off, tossing it to the floor. I positioned her on top of the bed, pulling her shorts off. She was pantyless. I stared at her mound, which happened to be bare and obviously waxed, while Riana's warning about Chelsea's lack of sex over the last year rang loud and clear in my thoughts.

For the first time ever, I saw Chelsea fully naked, even though the rumors and blogs thought differently. She was fucking perfect and I couldn't wait to satisfy my urge. My shirt and sweatpants were off in seconds.

I climbed on top of her, placing kisses all over. "Oh no, Sean, I want all of you right now. So take those fucking boxers *off*," she demanded. I removed them as she ordered. I continued to lave my tongue over her mouth, gently biting down on her bottom lip. The pecks continued to her neck and down to her navel. Chelsea glared with a longing that I knew *only* I could satisfy.

My fingers went in her nice and slow as she sung, "Ooh, Sean, mmm." I continued to fondle her, using my free fingers to touch other parts of her insides. I licked every crease until I went for what I knew she wanted. My hands slid under her butt while pulling her closer. My tongue devoured her insides while simultaneously fucking her. She became senseless. Her eyes half open but completely on me. Her moaning was so instrumental that at any moment I felt I could give in.

"Sean it's been a while and you gon make me cum like this," she squirmed.

I looked up while talking to her pussy, "Calm down baby, try to hold on." My rock hard dick was ready to go in her, like ten minutes ago but I only cared to pleasure her at the moment.

I pushed her legs back towards her head, origami style. My initial thought was to dive in but the spread of her lips looked too enticing. Instead, I kept her in position, with one hand keeping her legs back. My face went down for the pudding. She melted and I was there to clean it all up.

The sweet aroma that accompanied her pie was tantalizing and I loved how sweet she tasted. I could tell this would become an addiction of mine and I would be more than willing to endure a mouthful of cavities if I had to.

I knew she would climax soon so I pulled out a condom and slid it on. I laid on top of her, pushing my dick in gradually. I only had the tip in, teasing her a bit. I refused to let it fully go in but then she straddled me so hard making me fall deep into her. "Fuck, you feel so fucking good!" Her tightness was nothing to be reckoned with. I was convinced then that she hadn't had anything in her, EVER.

I stroked her while caressing her face. I progressed gently at first but it felt so warm that I couldn't maintain. I could feel my peak coming so I started pounding aggressively. Her hips below me moved in sync with my attack. As I kept going, she lapped my mouth, like she was starving.

"I fucking love you, Chelsea, I've been in love with you for quite some time." I saw tears rolling down her face. I kept pushing while slowing down.

"No keep going," she moaned. So I went full force. "Uhh, uhh, I-I-I'm—," she screamed and started shaking. I could feel her walls contracting and liquifying. Then seconds later I released with her.

We'd fallen asleep. It was dark in the room, glancing up I noticed the time, 3:12 am. Damn, I never anticipated spending the night. In my arms, Chelsea slept peacefully and the beauty she possessed held me captive.

A while later I got up and marched into the kitchen, hungry as hell. Anytime I came to her house I was welcome to do whatever, whenever, and the same rule applied for Chelsea.

I whipped up some scrambled eggs and cheese, bacon, toast, and sausages. Then I noticed she had pancake batter, and decided I'd cooked that too. Chelsea always told me the way to her heart was food, so how could I go wrong?

A naked Chelsea walked in, "Wow, you up super early." The revelation of her bare canvas had my nerves all fucked up. Her perky round ass and titties sent an electric current straight through me. It was as if she had super powers.

Looking at the refrigerator door, I noticed the display, 4:20 am. "Yeah, I wanted to cook. I got here a little after six yesterday and obviously, we haven't eaten since."

Rubbing her nipples seductively she replied, "Yeah because you were too busy eating *me* last night!" My dick shot up instantly, leaving no room for breakfast. Instead, we devoured each other for the remainder of the morning.

CHAPTER FIVE

CHELSEA

IT HAD BEEN a long day on set and I couldn't wait to get home to settle down. But that didn't change the fact that I had a great day on set with Dorien either.

Dorien was the latest actor in every film and show. He broke new barriers that hadn't been attained by any within his age range in the industry. I enjoyed some music on my break when I heard an intern talking on the phone, "Girl, yeah, Dorien is on set today and he is so fine. His fine ass can have me anyway he wants. And he looks like Michael B. Jordan, hell yes, that's the move." These girls were a trip but she was right, he looked exactly like him.

Dorien and I had been on several dates over the past few months, but I told him we could only be friends because I couldn't see myself with anyone at the time. I half-explained what happened with Randall and of course, he thought I was tripping, considering me and Randall were together before he blew up. But thinking about it now, the only man I felt that I could trust was Sean since we were honest with one another. But that nigga dick been in so many hoes that I don't think I could fathom the thought.

Dorien interrupted my thoughts, "Damn you did that today! You really helped bring my character out. Thank you." I gave him a wink and smiled. "Yeah, you were great too, but I still have one more scene to do." He looked at me and frowned, "Oh, ok.... I was thinking we could catch a late movie or something?"

"I don't know. Did you not see the tabloids and all the speculations circulating about us?" He knew where I was going with this.

"Let me take you somewhere private and we can go from there." Hearing his words made me feel bad but I knew this wasn't what I wanted.

Later that evening, Dorien and I pulled up to a hotel. I thought, "What the fuck we 'bout to do here?" But I stayed silent to see what he had up his sleeves. I was still sore from the loving Sean gave me that there was no way in hell I needed any more than that.

His chauffeur opened our door and Dorien got out. Seconds later he grabbed my hands and I followed. We walked into the double sliding doors that read, *"Hollywood Roosevelt Hotel."* It was empty, with no sign of anyone. Then a few steps later, there stood a sign, *"The Spare Room."* I remained still, having a full-blown conversation in my head at this point. "Hmmm, what spare room? The Spare room my ass. Who the fuck this nigga think he is? Yea, this dude could have spared my time and left me alone." Then I snapped back into reality as we walked in.

The elegance and picturesque features of the place seemed unreal. I continued to observe the earth tone color decor and the accented walls. There a bar existed with several bowling lanes, a section to head out for go-kart, laser tag, and different areas to play different games, such as dominoes, connect four and etcetera.

I felt confused, I had never seen a bowling alley with board games. The place really reminded me of a kid's fun spot but for adults. The privacy this place had was surreal. We had a special hostess to make sure our night ran smooth, from bottle and food service, making sure the temperature stayed to par in the room and even went as far as removing any extra clothing, such as sweaters. The lady deserved a big tip and Dorien didn't come up short on that at all.

"I come here every so often with my boys and we love it. But I reserved it for only us, so we can have a good time and celebrate you being here in LA. I know you like privacy so no one will bother us for the next few hours," Dorien explained. I smiled and at that moment he made me realize, a man will treat you right when he wants too. This dude had taken me so many places and he showed me a good time every time.

Our night turned out great after I whooped his ass in a few games. But my focus wasn't at all on him since Sean had been texting and calling throughout the evening. "Dorien, you have so many girls that want you, but yet you continue to pursue me, what's up?" He looked up, stunned by my question.

"I don't know, you do something to me. You don't chase me, you focus on what you want and that's it. I think it's nice that you're about your business, instead of everyone else's. I have been feeling you since I saw you on the Blair Project, I just never said anything." I was flattered and squeezed his hands with appreciation.

"Well Dorien, I really enjoyed this night and thank you for being thoughtful of my feelings."

"Anytime Chelsea... But hey, I was wondering if you wanted to be my date at the Film & Music Awards? That's one of the biggest events here in LA and everyone that's somebody is supposed to be there. As a bonus, I'm nominated for a few things."

"I would but I haven't figured everything out yet. I know I'm going because I'm supposed to be presenting an award and I have been nominated for best-supporting actress."

His eyes lit up, "What? That's huge. Damn, I didn't even know. Congratulations."

I wasn't all that hyped about it until then. "I haven't told anybody personally. You're the first to know." Dorien seemed surprised to hear that. He hugged me and proceeded to kiss my lips but I turned my face, having his lip to fall on my cheek."

"It's like that?" He said embarrassed.

"No, I don't want to start anything that's all." But the truth was I wanted Sean.

As we walked out of the place there were tons of cameras. In my heart, I knew if Sean saw this, he would assume the worse and the rest would be history. But then I remembered, I was single and free to do whatever I wanted.

My focus shifted back to the onlookers and all I wanted to do is disappear. Dorien pushed the cameramen out of the way and covered us as much as possible. Moments like this made me realize how much I was starting to hate LA.

♪♪ *"Moneybag, moneybag...,"* blasted while I walked onto the gated property. This home was a sight to see. It housed ten bedrooms, twelve baths, two pools, a basketball court and I could go on and on. If I'd never been here before, I would have been drooling. But over the past few years, I had spent endless nights here hanging out with Sean.

"Girl look at all these people? Sean sure knows how to throw a party. He almost outdid me." I listened to Riana talk and joke about some of the guests. People stopped us to congratulate me on my new bookings, while people stopped Riana because... Hell, she's Riana!

Ri and I partied away. Being that it was a pool party, we weren't fully dressed and no one on the premises was either. I sported my all white, two-piece Gucci bathing suit with some matching flip-flops and a mesh top that barely covered my ass. Meanwhile, Riana had my exact outfit on but her two-piece swimsuit contained a thong bottom versus underwear. I wasn't mad because she did her thang and looked sexy doing it.

I noticed a few missed calls from Sean and decided to slip away from Riana for a sec.

"Where the fuck you think you going?" Riana inquired while grabbing my arms.

"Where you think?"

She eyed me and smiled, "Oooh you so nasty, damn that man hit the spot for you huh? And you never finished telling me the details but I'll wait cause it's obvious you about to go try to get some more of that dingalinggggg..."

"No hunty! Let's rephrase that because dingalinggggg sounds small and I promise you there's nothing small on Sean at all. His dick is thick and hearty, with plenty of hang time," I laughed with my tongue out, dancing, throwing my hands up simultaneously.

Ri cried with laughter... But she knew I was serious.

Alone, I walked towards the side door entrance to the house. People seemed to be having fun but it felt like they were eyeing me. Or maybe I was paranoid since I knew the gossip that circulated about us.

I entered what he called 'the cave.' This portion of the house contained a theater, bowling alley and anything you could think of entertainment wise. It was dark so I assumed he was on the other side of the place, or hell somewhere else in the house. I called his phone a few times but no answer. I decided to take the elevator to his bedroom. Coming off, I heard him moving around but I hadn't made it into the room yet.

My eyes widened as I saw him moving across his room with nothing on. I saw his well-built ass first. As he turned I saw what I'd named 'Long Sean Silver.' I would've turned away but since we already crossed that path I figured what's the point.

I swear he knew I was looking, he took his time in all he did, but the gestures he did towards his dick caused the hairs on my neck to stand.

"Oh! Wow, you out in the open butt ass neked!" He laughed at my comment but didn't get dressed.

Instead, his fine ass strutted my way, biting his bottom lip. "Did you think about what I asked you? About us?" Are we gonna make it official, Chelsea?"

I did think about it, but fear of what comes with a man that has a celebrity status crept into my heart. Would he do me like Randall and cheat then get a girl pregnant? Six years of being with Randall, you would think he wouldn't put our relationship in jeopardy but that was so far from the truth.

I expressed with passion, "Yes, I thought about it but I don't know if I can trust you. I don't want to go through what I did with Randall. I am scared to try with you."

He walked over to his massive bed that could easily fit twenty and sat down. He held a stern look on his face. "Ok, but what makes you think a regular nigga won't do the same? Hell, many niggas cheat and money doesn't have shit to do with it. Girls are drawn to me, true enough, but when I'm in a relationship I know how to do right. I have learned a lot from my past mistakes." I could tell he was upset with me but he kept it cool.

"Then I hear all the gossip about me being with certain people with money—."

He shut me down real quick as he stood up and yelled, "Fuck what they think! The people that matter knows the real Chelsea Renee Collins. You so worried about these non-factors that don't give a shit about you or me. They wake up and want to have something to say and make you miserable just like them. They want something to talk about. Don't you understand that? If you worried about that now then how are you gonna deal when you really get big? I'mma tell you this, I ain't saying you have to be with me but always remember.... Don't live for anybody but yourself. At the end of the day, you do have people that love you but no one has your back like you do, so fuck them and be happy!"

This man delivered a whole speech and then some. It was obvious I got under his skin. But he had some valid views.

"Just give me some time to really work with myself and pray about it. But let me ask you something, if we make it official then what? You have so many girls in your phone, then you're touring... It's a lot for me."

"I'll cut them off if that's what you're trying to figure out. And touring is nothing. If you have free time you can always travel with me. You could even consider staying here with Cam if you want. With you, I'm willing to change everything in my life." His revelation shocked me but I couldn't see myself staying in his house since I loved my space. At least that's what I thought at the moment.

Our conversation went for a turn as I watched Sean Silver grow long and strong. I decided to take control, but first I observed the scenery of people having fun below us from

Sean's room. His room had floor to ceiling windows and I needed to make sure they wouldn't see us.

"Hey, do you have any rubbers?" I asked while still looking out the window.

"Yeah."

I stood on the opposite side of his bed, removing my mesh top slowly in front of him as if it were a striptease. Gradually making my way to him, my top came off. And I purposely took my panties off last. I bent all the way over with my ass in his face so he could see my insides from the back.

My knees suddenly hit the bed. I assumed he got on his knees as I felt pressure from behind. I felt his tongue smothering my insides. *"Whew*, Sean, I can get used to this." I *wanted* him inside of me, I *needed* him inside of me. I pushed him onto the bed and got on top. Positioning myself directly on top of his shaft, the outpour of fluids allowed him to glide in with no constraints. His thickness pulsated causing a stir of excitement which made me want more control. I rode the hell out of him, and I promise the Kentucky Derby ain't have shit on me. *"Shiiiit*, Chelsea, *fuuuck*, this feeeeels——sooo good." He got hostile and the perspiration continued profusely from the both of us dampening the sheets. The impulsiveness our tongues shared was a reminder of the desire we had to take each other in.

He slung me off of him and positioned my legs on his shoulder as he propelled in and out. "Deeper baby, shiiiit, yes! I want all of it," I moaned. Tilting my hips up, he dived deeper, hitting my hotspot. I jerked, squeezing the sheets in my hands while clutching down on my lips. The sounds of our bodies crashing together excited me and caused me to climax and collapse.

I could tell Sean held out until I finished. When he saw I made the journey he flipped me over, propping me on my hands and knees. Thrusting from the back, he was out in less than a minute with a loud roar.

As we laied there out of breath, something came over me. At that moment, I felt the urge to tell him yes to taking a chance on us. I rested my head on his chest as he leaned in with his luscious lips, sinking into my skin, "If you were to get your act right, then you could have all of this anytime you want it." I looked at him crazy because in my mind I already had all of it.

CHAPTER SIX

SEAN

HAPPINESS OVERFLOWED WITHIN ME, and I could only thank God for that. I was touring, got to see family in my free time, and had a quick break to party with a few friends. Being back in LA for forty-eight hours gave me the boost I needed.

I slipped on my black and gold swim shorts to head outside to my guests as Chelsea followed behind. This girl had me gone mentally. Ever since our first encounter, she's been all I could reflect on. I would blame it on lust, but I knew better. Since the day I met her I'd been engrossed in the person she was. The more time we spent together, the more I learned of her genuine ways.

"It's good to see you two come out of hibernation. Did you get lost, Chelsea?" Riana questioned, and after not hearing an answer, she turned to me, "Or did your dick happen to slip inside of her?"

I cackled so damn hard, I could have peed on myself. "Riana, you gotta take that up with yo friend. She the one that came up and started harassing me while I was trying to get out here to y'all. She manhandled me and everything."

Chelsea jumped in to defend herself, "Sean whatever. You know what's up, and Ri, I know you not talking, don't make me call your ass out."

Ri rolled her eyes and kept teasing.

We had to tone it down as people were starting to look at us. There had to be about two hundred people in attendance and everyone focused on their own thing. Some were swimming, hooping, eating and everything else in between.

A few hours went by as the sun started setting. Benji, Dion and the rest of my boys were playing spades when I walked up. We chopped it up while drinking.

One of my boys yelled, "Sean, there are some baddies over here. I think I might slide into something tonight."

I shook my head and replied, "Go ahead my boy, you know I ain't mad at that."

Then Benji started clowning, "Sean, please, you already know your ass ain't bout that life right now because of Chelsea over there. So, you know ain't no fun for you tonight. Your ass is on *clank clank,* we might as well throw away the keys."

I personally didn't see shit funny. "I'm not in any relationship, I can come and go as I please. Besides, Chelsea doing her thang. But if she does decide to make it work then yeah, I'll settle down. In the meantime, I do what I want." Benji and the boys looked at me with no response. They were pissing me off, but I got over it.

"Riana let me holla at you right quick," Benji yelled. Riana rolled her eyes and didn't move. But a few minutes later she appeared.

"What Benji? I'm catching up with the girls." Benji stalled thinking of the best way to approach her with his proposition, "I'm tryna see if you needed a date to the Film and Music Awards?"

Everyone was quiet while waiting on Riana's response, "Nah, thanks for offering, but Chelsea is attending with me and with our busy schedules it's too late to change the game plan. Besides Benji, you might not be old enough to ride this ride!" Then she had the nerve to wink at Benji after saying that!

"Really Ri, you only a year and a half older." After going back and forth, Riana went back to doing whatever and the boys went hunting for females.

As things died down, Chelsea told me she was going inside and for me to watch Riana since she had been drinking. I did just that but noticed something weird. Everyone had left the party except my boys and a few of Chelsea's friends. I didn't know where Benji went and I didn't go looking for him either. But where was Riana?

I moved inside to double check on Chelsea but to my surprise, I heard some moaning in the foyer area. "I thought you didn't fuck with younger niggas? Take this shit!" I couldn't believe what I'd heard. That damn Benji and Riana were at it. I wasn't gonna hate and mess things up, at least I knew Riana was safe but from the sound of it Benji was fucking her brains out.

Chelsea headed down the steps, as I headed up. I tried to turn her around so she didn't walk in on her friend. "Why are you looking crazy Sean?"

"Nothing just want you back upstairs with me."

"No, I promised Ri I would be right back"

"Well, she talking to Benji."

Chelsea gave me a look and obviously, she knew her friend well. "Mhmm, talking to Benji? Well, there's nothing wrong with that."

"Let's go upstairs so I can taste you."

"Sean you can taste me later, you're hiding something. Did you forget how well I know you? Besides, we don't lie to each other remember?"

"Ok go," I said, making sure she knew I was irritated.

Pure silence filled the room then about a minute later she walked back up and stared at me like I did something wrong. "What, what I do? I ain't tell her to spread her legs for Benji. That's your friend. Let her bust it open if she wants. Hell, I'm trying to be like them upstairs with you."

She walked off rolling her eyes. "Babe, she is super drunk though. And she's in a relationship so this shouldn't be. You know I don't usually care since they both are adults, but I don't want her messing up a good relationship?" Hearing her concern for her friend made me love Chelsea more. She was always thoughtful and looked out for those she loved.

We decided to walk outside to the pool area and talk.

Then Riana and Benji joined us. "How are you feeling tonight?" Chelsea joked.

"Fucking amazing! I didn't know Benji young ass knew some things. I don't know, I may have to try that shit out again when I'm not tipsy." We all laughed while Benji seemed embarrassed.

"I tried to tell you my dick game ain't shit to play with girl." Riana smiled and rested on Benji's lap as we all continued conversing.

"My man Cam, what's up?" I said while dapping him up. Chelsea and I decided to do a game night at her place with her son Cam. Usually, I would have the two young men that I mentored with me, and Chelsea and Cam would come to meet us out somewhere to hang. Tonight, they wouldn't be with me, but I hoped this wouldn't seem weird to Cam. Truth be told, I wouldn't want him to think Chelsea and I were more than friends.

"This new place looks good Chelsea. I see you made your LA home just as comfortable as Atlanta."

"Yeah, I guess. I think I need a few more things but this will do. I'm just glad Cam is here with me on his break."

Her place was nestled in a nice neighborhood in West Hollywood. It surprised me to see her move there since the traffic was crazy. A ten-minute drive could turn into forty-minutes, bumper to bumper, easily.

Her new high-rise condo consisted of two bedrooms and

two baths. The view was amazing, no matter what part of the home you were in. You could see the mountains and buildings from virtually anywhere in the condo. The view from her master bathroom showcased the Olympic size pool and hot tub area. I started thinking what all I could do to her and in what positions, but then she snapped me back into reality, "Boy, what are you thinking about? It better be about me."

After getting a tour of her new home, I realized Cam had his own plans for us. "Sean, come on so I can kick your butt on this 2K18 and if you don't get tired of getting beat then we can play Fortnite."

"Cam you don't want me to embarrass you in front of your momma. Keep playing and I'm a have to record this and expose you to your friends."

We started playing and sure enough, this boy was really good. I was still up by two points but he kept up. I always cared about Cam. The past four years I would always call him and send him gifts for his birthday and Christmas. Last Christmas I gave him a gift card to use at GameStop the contained several hundred dollars, since he emphasized his love of video games. Luckily, Randall never took offense.

After a few rounds, Chelsea came in with boxes that read, Blaze Pizza. "YES!" Cam yelled.

Blaze pizza was always a favorite for me and Chelsea so I wasn't surprised. Blaze lets you customize your pizza from the sauce to the toppings. So, it shocked me to see my pizza was exactly how I liked it. "Chelsea you know me too well. This pizza hit the spot," I mumbled while chewing.

"Yeah, same here mom."

"Ok, y'all boys done left me out of what I planned to be a game night for all of us. So now what am I left to do?"

Cam and I looked at each other and guffawed. "Sorry mom, I just had to show Sean who was the man. But you can pick what we do next."

Chelsea looked at the time and smiled, "Yeah, sounds like it's time for you to go to bed, it's 11:29."

Cam somehow talked us into watching the movie, "Pete's Dragon." Chelsea laid on the couch with her back on the armrest, with her legs spread across, like there weren't two other bodies. Cam sat in between her legs while reclining back. Poor me, I was stuck at the end.

Cam had his thick cashmere cover swaddling us. Since Chelsea had her feet all over, that allowed me to rub them while the movie played. She looked at me while her eyes begged for more. While gripping her foot with my hand, I applied pressure to the middle of her foot with my thumb. I glided my thumb up and down. After I noticed her moving a little too much, assuming her centerpiece was on fire, I stopped.

Finally, Cam fell asleep. Without a word, I picked him up and carried him into his bedroom and tucked him in. I was a man with no kids but here I was attending to this boy that I honestly wouldn't mind having in my life forever. After tonight I noticed he was far from a cock-blocking kid. Most kids act up if you near their mom but not him. Then again, he did know me and had no suspicions of us.

Walking out of his room and closing the door behind me, Chelsea stood. "Thanks for showing Cam a good night." She leaned in brushing her tongue along my bottom lip, sucking on it nice and slow. My hands slid down to her backside, gripping and squeezing it tight as I brought her into an intimate embrace.

I knew there wasn't much we could do since I remembered her mentioning being on her cycle earlier while she talked to Riana. But that didn't stop me from teasing her.

As our tongues fought, I slowly walked her backward, towards her bedroom. Locking the door behind us, I laid her on the bed and went for her neck. My fingers gently massaged the back of her head. "Mmmmm, I love you," she whispered.

"I love you too, Chelsea.

"Tonight isn't a good night to—."

I cut her off, "Don't worry about tonight, go clean yourself up then come lay with me. Let's do like we used to do and have fun. Everything is still the same you know? We just made it a little complicated with the sex and emotions. But you are still my best friend."

She smiled and headed to the restroom. "Sean, come here and talk to me." That's what I loved about her. We were so cool that we could talk while she did anything and the same remained true even after we slept together.

"Why you acting like you ain't never seen me on the toilet before?"

I gave her an awkward stare, "I've seen you like this but I also know exactly what that ass looks like now. I guess I can stop fantasizing now."

We laughed.

There were times in the past when she would be showering and I'd be in there telling her a story. When she would finish, I respected her enough to know to leave out and go into another room.

I'll never forget the night I had sex with a girl named Desiree. I guess I was so fucked up that I started talking shit and telling her why I could never be with her. Desiree thought she had the upper hand by kicking me out of her house without my clothes and without a ride since I got dropped off by my driver who wouldn't be back until the morning.

So, I called Chelsea and Desiree overheard the conversation. Desiree said something like, "Oh you calling your main bitch, huh? Tell her to come pick you up and bring you some clothes since you always with her. You always riding her and want another bitch to just be there while you have your cake too. Hell, why you fucking me when you could be fucking her? I bet she can't help you tonight since she's in Atlanta."

Little did she know, Chelsea was in town for a gig and she also knew the code to get into my house if there was ever an emergency. Within thirty minutes, Chelsea had been to my house to get me some clothes and was pulling into Desiree's driveway. She still wouldn't give me my clothes but I didn't trip because I walked out of her house just as I was, in my Polo boxers. As I kept stepping, I shot her a bird, "Nice knowing ya, oh and thanks for the head, I appreciate ya!"

Chelsea fussed the whole ride home. She said it wasn't the fact of what just went down but I have to still respect women. I did and always respected women but I didn't have respect for Desiree.

I believe that's why people never believed me when I said I never smashed Chelsea before. We were too close in people's eyes but yet she and I knew the truth.

CHAPTER SEVEN

CHELSEA

FLASHES OF LIGHTS flickered everywhere when Riana and I stepped foot out the vehicle. I angled my head to the side so she could hear me while moving forward, "Ri, I'm so nervous! I can't believe I was even nominated."

She gripped my arm closer to her, "Bitch believe it because you got a thousand more coming. We're going to shine together. With or without me, I know you gon do that shit. Just know I'm here for you no matter what."

I inhaled a deep breath while looking up to the Microsoft sign on the building. I felt the flutters in my stomach and knew I needed to channel my alter ego.

The host and reporters interviewed everyone on the red carpet. "Chelsea, you look stunning darling! I love your dress. Who are you wearing?"

"Thanks! This is a Valentino dress, very last minute for me but I love it."

"So, you're here with your best friend Riana. Are there any surprises that we should look forward to during the show?"

"I don't know, I guess you'll have to watch and see."

The reporter got a good laugh out of that. "Right, well I hope you take home the Best Supporting Actress Award."

"Me too! I'm overwhelmed by all of the support and thankful to even have been nominated." I laughed right along with her.

We finished the red carpet and headed inside. I was glad to be seated in the front section of the venue, but I noticed the seating arrangements might cause some issues. Riana and I were placed next to each other but I noticed Dorien's name to the left of my seat. And behind me, Sean and Benji's name appeared.

Thirty minutes remained before the show started and everyone was mingling. I noticed Sean first, wearing a black and red Armani suit with some black loafers. But the red blazer was the highlight of the outfit. *Shiiiit*, he looked like a full course meal, I thought. For once he kept it really simple by only showcasing his big-faced gold Patek watch. Instantly, I craved his manhood. Thoughts of his naked masculine body flooded my thoughts causing juices to run down into my panties. I yearned for him and couldn't fathom not having him in me.

Before I could talk to other people, Sean invaded my personal space by pushing his chest into me, his deep baritone voice projected, "Look at you, you're so gorgeous." With our hands interlocking I hissed, "You don't look too bad yourself, Sean B."

I could tell he was turned on and wanted me too. He squinted his eyes as he tried to figure me out. His body obviously had a mind of its own because I felt something hit my navel. Sliding my tongue across my teeth, I shot a quick look at his erection, "Did I make you do that?" Sean guffawed a bit and brushed it towards me more which let me know he wasn't letting up. I gazed around the area hoping no one noticed, but hurried and changed the subject before we became fodder for the gossip blogs.

I told him about the seating arrangements but he didn't care. He said the people who arrange the shows always found ways to stir up a commotion.

The show started with Tiffany Haddish as this year's host. She was funny as hell and I couldn't wait to meet her. She was live and the crowd had no choice but to be too.

Sean tapped me on the shoulder and whispered, "I'm about to perform, you can come hang with me in the back if you want?" I told him no, but if I changed my mind I'll find my way back there. He nodded and left his seat leaving me with Dorien since Riana was backstage getting ready to perform as well.

"You look beautiful tonight Chelsea," Dorien said while grabbing my hands. "Thanks," I replied, while slowly removing my hands from him.

I knew my time was close to head backstage since I had to present an award, but then my thoughts were interrupted by

Tiffany Haddish's scream. "Let's put our hands up for Sean B!" The crowd roared with anticipation.

His hype man came out first and Sean followed behind, but this time his suit was off. He'd changed into some black jogger pants and a black sleeveless shirt revealing all his muscles and tattoos. The crowd went crazy. He had all the people on their feet as they rocked to the beat and they sang every word.

I had a great view of his performance since I sat on the second row in the center. I was like his hype woman in the crowd. I noticed Dorien observing me but he knew what was up. After a while, Dorien stood up vibing right along with me.

Nearing the end of his performance, Sean shouted out a lot of people and became a little emotional.

"I can go on and on tonight with you all, but I want to be real about some stuff. I've had a rough year! Many of you don't know but I lost one of my closest friends to cancer earlier this year and I also lost my grandmother. But what I'm saying is life is too short, and if you know like I know then you all should live and go after your dreams. Tell your loved ones you love them. Don't let life pass you by without living and loving. One thing that's promised to us all is death, but what do we leave behind? Are we leaving enemies, hate, regret? We all should leave love, compassion, hope, purpose or whatever it is you want. So live for today and live with no regrets! Peace!"

The crowd went crazy with applause after Sean's performance.

"You ready? It's almost time to do the award presentation," Sienna, the stage manager asked as she slid next to me in the empty seat. Sean had just walked off the stage and people were moving about trying to hurry before the break was up.

I smiled staring at the headset she rocked over her tight curls. "Sienna you got her?" A deep voice sounded out of her walkie talkie. "Copy," she countered.

"Come on girl before they come hunting me down," I giggled while lifting from my seat and following her to prepare for my five minutes in the spotlight.

I made my way onto the stage to present the award for the Video of the Year but felt uneasy with Lexi's presence.

"Man, it's so great to see you all having such a great time tonight. Are you ready to find out who won Video of the Year?" I yelled and the crowd cheered uncontrollably.

"Well we know who's definitely getting Sean tonight," Lexi said through the mic that we shared.

She was throwing shade since Sean performed his hit song "Confess," which highlighted our journey together. The little thirty second snippet caused many to look in my direction but I didn't care, he never acknowledged that it was me he was referencing.

I smiled while trying to keep my composure, but before I could say anything else, she barked again.

"I'm sure whoever wins this award didn't have to ummm," Lexi paused with a smirk.

"Lexi I'm glad you're feeling entertained however, I'm unsure of where you're headed with this. I can't attest that you even know yourself. So, if you don't mind, I think we should present this award because we are not the center of focus tonight," I growled then *pointed to the award paper results,* "they are."

The crowd applauded and I could tell Lexi was embarrassed but I was sick of her.

After giving the award, I headed backstage to check in with Riana.

"I woulda fucked that bitch up, off top! It's ok though, we gon get her ass," Riana screamed while opening the door to exit towards the stage.

My words barely rolled out my mouth to respond when they called her to the stage. "We have Riana coming to the stage," Tiffany shouted to the audience.

Riana was grooving to the beat when Lexi walked passed me and I couldn't help but to redirect my steps towards her. I cornered her, trying to keep the attention at bay. I placed one hand to her shoulder but she moved back flipping her hair and turned up her mouth, "Don't touch me."

I gasped with frustration and pointed my finger at her, "Listen bitch. I don't step out of character often but I need you to understand where I'm coming from." I lost it at that point, but was still cool enough. "I'm not sure what you were insinuating out there but I know I've worked very hard to get where I am now. For you, I can't quite say the same since your reputation in the industry is long. And I agree with you, we do know who's going to be with Sean tonight and it won't be you."

Lexi seemed flustered as she walked off but then turned back around and stuck her middle finger up at me. I strutted towards her when Sean walked in between us and pulled me away.

He pushed me against the wall gently and kept his hands on my arms, "Chelsea, why you letting her get under your skin? That's not even like you." I looked down at the floor because true enough that wasn't me. But I was starting to dislike her more and more by the day.

Sean tilted my head with his finger, not caring that there were plenty of workers going back and forth around us. Back-stage was just as busy to me as it was in the audience. He leaned in closer with his chest rising up and down against me and remained still for a second before whispering, "I love the fuck out of you girl."

I needed to get out of his presence because the feelings were too overwhelming. I wanted to give him all of me right there but kept my composure and remained neutral.

Plenty of videos and pictures circulated over the years of us that seemed intimate, but what we had going at this very moment was real and there was nothing innocent about it.

CHAPTER EIGHT

SEAN

RIANA CAME OUT OF NOWHERE, sweat dripping from her hair. She motioned for Chelsea to come her way. I kissed her cheek as she moved out of my arms. They looked to each other smiling.

I knew I was tripping. I was being bold as fuck knowing damn well Chelsea wasn't ready to reveal anything about us. I was stopped by a tap on my shoulder. "My nigga... About time you and Chelsea make it official. I'm happy for y'all," Shooter commented.

I dapped him up and was glad as hell to see him. Even though he and Chelsea worked closely together, I never thought anything about it. Their established relationship helped form a bond between him and I. Not to mention, our friendship led to a few hit songs.

"Man, she ain't never give me an official answer, but we'll

see. But that song up there was specifically for her and I'm sure she understood the subliminal message."

"Subliminal? Nigga, everyone knows you basically asked her to be more than a friend. But I rock with it though." I was surprised by his statement but left it alone. I guess he could sense my hesitation and shifted subjects. "We need to lay another track down Sean. It's been a minute."

"Yeah we gon do that," I replied back while checking my phone. My phone was going crazy from all the feedback on the show. From the look of things, it was all good.

"How about I hit you up within a week and see what we can do? I do have a new album I'm working on," Shooter said and I nodded my head, "Cool."

A few more people stopped and talked to me. Then Dorien came up, "Can we talk for a sec?" I looked at him while walking to the corner where there were couches and flatscreens that broadcasted the live show.

"What's up?" I said, while throwing my hands up but had a slight grin.

"I wanted to tell you that I didn't know you and Chelsea had anything going on and I don't want you to think I disrespected you by coming at her or taking her out." With a scowl on my face, I continued listening but I was a little annoyed. He really didn't owe me any explanation.

"And to clarify any rumors, I never had sex with her either. I just took her out on a few dates and we kicked it. She's different than a lot of these chicks, and I think you're lucky to have her. Congrats on everything." After talking he walked off. He never gave me a chance to say anything but his comments did make me appreciate Chelsea even more.

The night progressed so fast and because I was having such a good time I didn't want it to end. Naomi Blasingame, top Journalist from Take Note walked up to me with her mic and cameraman, wanting my input on the show. She asked me what made me open up tonight during my performance?

"My speech about apologizing for my wrongdoings and love is important to me because I want a clean slate. I want a new beginning with every new relationship I enter into, personal and business. This night was a revelation that you create what you want and the more positive the better." The lady asked more questions but I knew it was time for me to head back to my seat out in the audience.

I could tell we were on commercial break as backstage got busy all of a sudden. But then I heard, "We are getting ready to announce the winner for Best Supporting Actress."

I quickly went by the stage opening in case Chelsea won the award. My heart pounded in hopes for her to win. I tried to spot where she was but it seemed she had already made it back to her seat. Then I noticed people walking onto the stage and I assumed the time had come.

"Man, this is a tough decision because everyone on this list was so amazing. But we were only allowed to choose one. And the winner is...... Chelsea Collins!" I cheered and clapped along with the crowd.

She made her way to the stage while her hand covered her mouth. She seemed ecstatic. I could see her hand shaking, but she managed to keep it together. Her hair looked perfect in the up-do style which was very flattering. I watched her hips sway left to right and noticed just how perfect God created her in each and every way.

With a trembling voice, she started to speak, "I am so honored to be where I am today. I dreamed of this but never expected this to come so fast for me. I ummm— I want to thank God first and foremost. I have prayed so much and asked God to guide me in which he saw best. Also, my family and friends that have shown me so much support and encouragement. There have been many times when I felt like quitting, but their voices pushed me forward. I don't know where I would be without them. And I thank each and every one of you and the people who voted for me."

With the crowd on their feet cheering for her I observed her walking off the stage towards me. She was sexy as fuck and I couldn't wait to tear her ass up. Once she made it to me, we were arm in arm, headed towards the dressing area. She firmly grasped my hands and started expressing herself, "Babe, I thought about what you said, you were right. Why care about what people think? The people who know me best know my ways and I shouldn't be concerned with anyone's opinions. I'm so glad you kept it real with me and that's why I want you in my life, forever, if possible. I don't want no other man but you."

I smirked at her, "Is that right?"

"Yes, Sean. You have shown me a lot of support and love and that's why I stand here to say yes, yes I would love to see where our relationship goes from here. I love you."

My heart exploded. All I wanted more than anything was

to make it to our destination. And finally, I saw the sign on my dressing room door, "*Sean B.*"

The door barely closed when I pushed Chelsea against the wall. The adrenaline rush from both of us caused a catastrophe. We floated on cloud nine. Mouth to mouth, our tongues glided against one another. Her hands were behind my head as I gripped her, sliding my hand up underneath her dress. I could feel her thong and somehow managed to tear them off her.

"Damn baby I love you so much," Chelsea yelped out of breath with her mouth covering mine. I pulled back and nipped at her neck then put her down. I stared into her eyes, letting her take me in. "Don't look at me like that, I don't wanna cut up in here," she purred. That was the worst thing she could have whispered. I immediately bent her over the couch, removing everything off her. I stood there admiring her bare ass. I trailed my lip from one ass cheek to the other. I pulled a condom out of my pocket and dropped my pants down while I slid inside of her, forcing every bit of me in.

Her opening was dripping wet, giving my shaft a bath. Hell, a bath was an understatement. Shit, I was flooded out by her juices. Swishing noises filled the room.

She moaned begging me to go faster. I did just that until she ordered me to stop moving and not touch her. She wanted to do the work herself. I stood there staring at her bent over spine, watching her reinsert me inside of her opening from the back. She was so forceful that she had to hold on to a table while throwing her ass back. I wanted to pull her hair or grab the back of her neck but I had to endure the urge of not touching her. She worked the hell out my dick!

She thrust in and out, with every few seconds of changing patterns. Throwing her ass back I could handle but some way my back ended up against the wall which allowed both of her hands to hit the floor, and voila her feet planted onto the wall. "Shiiiit, baby," I groaned. She ravished the shit out me and best believe regardless of the position, she took in every inch. I was in awe.

Still, in position she played a game of hide and seek, allowing me to watch my shaft go in and out. I was only allowed to hold onto her sides, so for control, I started spanking that ass. She maintained her grip on both the wall and floor and finally I couldn't stand there.

Moving my hands to her waist, I lifted her up. I stroked her from the back while she remained in a straight angle, standing up but her feet hadn't hit the floor. Having full power was more like it but she had a rebuttal, "Babe I was supposed to be in control, I told you not to touch," she screeched.

I kept her up, still banging her in, "I'm sorry Chels, I couldn't stay away. You know how good your pussy is?"

"Yeah! Ooh, ooh—and its—all yours."

Her walls contracted against my shaft and her facial expression displayed a feeling of ecstasy. She sang so proudly with no fear of others overhearing us.

"Ssshh! They probably can hear you." She didn't seem to

care at all, her moans only grew louder. But that turned me on more. I kept pumping and felt myself getting ready to release which caused me to get more aggressive with my strokes. She stopped me. "Don't nut yet baby."

I became motionless as she repositioned, having me to sit on the vanity chair. I pushed it against the wall and did as she said. She got on top of me but this time all I could see was her back and her derriere. She straddled me backward and that drove me silly.

She bounced up and down, swirling seductively still maintaining me inside of her. I was mesmerized. I watched her go up and down while she magically made my shaft disappear and reappear again. I started to grunt a bit and couldn't keep my own satisfaction together.

"Shiiiit, I can't hold on much longer," I growled in her ears. She became more forceful with her riding pattern and I could tell she was about to climax and seconds later she did.

After riding, she hopped off facing me. Enticingly moving her hips, she put her hands on her knees and dropped down in front of me. Only now, she confronted Long Sean Silver, who was standing straight up as confident as ever.

"Mhm, you didn't know I had it in me, huh? I like it nasty but I can't do what I really want in here." She licked her lips and took the condom off, inserting all of me inside her warm mouth. She gripped while sucking and performing a few tricks that I never knew existed. She was about that life; She talked to it, sucked it, and played with it until I couldn't hold on.

That's when I told her I was about to let loose. She opted

to keep going, signaling for me to do it. I thrust my hips up, causing me to go further in her mouth. I could feel me hitting against her throat, but her gag reflexes were able to handle all my girth. My eyes grew wider as I felt the blood rushing through me. Then she gripped my balls into her hands with a firm squeeze. I immediately released in her mouth and she seemed just as happy as I did.

She went into the restroom that was inside the dressing room to clean up. "Tonight has been one of the most memorable nights of my life. I never expected so much love. And I had so much fun." She started talking like she didn't just blow my fucking mind. If I didn't love her before, that moment confirmed it!

"I'm am so happy for you. You deserved everything tonight baby," I said to her while kissing her forehead.

A knock sounded through the door, "Are you in there Sean? And where's my best friend? I just need her for a quick second." Riana came to rescue her friend. I let her in because I was dressed and I'm sure Chelsea wouldn't mind.

I barely opened the door, when Riana came running inside only to see her friend in the bathroom.

"Mhm, with yo nasty ass. I hope y'all used a condom because you gon be dripping all over these folks chair if you didn't."

Chelsea looked up at her and smiled. They continued their talk as I gathered our belongings. I knew it wouldn't be long before the show ended but I wanted to make sure everything was together.

Another knock filled the door, this time Riana's dude

Santos stood on the other end. "What's up Sean? Don't mean to bother, but Riana said I could find her in here if I needed her." While laughing I let him in. Riana flew into his arms so damn quick. I could tell she really liked him and her whole persona changed once he walked in.

Chelsea and I observed them and I quickly understood why she didn't want Riana messing with Benji. But in my mind as a man it made me think how trifling women could be. Here she tongued him down and just a while back fucked my brother. I tried to not think about it though, we all make mistakes. Who was I to judge, I had done my dirt in the past too.

CHAPTER NINE

CHELSEA

THE NEXT FEW weeks consisted of great vibes. After the awards show I had more opportunities than ever. I now had shows that I co-starred on. I had another offer to host a show similar to the view and many companies reached out to see if I could be the face of their product. I was grateful for the opportunities headed my way.

I couldn't believe Sean and I were officially together. I still had my judgments but I took a leap of faith. Sean and I had been in constant communication despite him being on tour. I had to admit, the lack of physical intimacy with him bothered me a little bit.

"Hey zaddy, you calling early, it's eight am our time." I smiled while watching Sean on the phone.

"Yeah that's because it's the late or rather early over here, it's one am to be exact. Remember Japan is seventeen hours ahead of you." I completely forgot about the time difference.

But I was glad the phone worked long enough for me to see him.

I grinned thinking how far Sean's career had progressed. His presence was already established in the states but watching him work internationally reminded me of his success. He was touring between the world and I was ecstatic for him.

"How are you holding up? Do you need anything? Don't forget you can stay at my house. It's closer to where you will be doing your table read."

"Yeah, I know. I'll shoot you a text if I do, but more than anything I miss talking to you face-to-face," I said frowning.

"I'll see you sooner than you think. I mean this was a six-month tour and I only have two-months left. At least, I've seen you a lot in between." I knew he was right so I stopped nagging. We ended our conversation a while after.

I made it back on set for the first time since the awards show. It seemed awkward facing Dorien while working but he kept it professional and never made me feel uncomfortable. I even noticed some of the production workers treating me differently. They acted as if I was higher in status, now that I had an award. Despite the aggravation I felt, I eventually got used to it.

On my way home, I got a call from Randall and he sounded pissed. Something obviously struck his nerve and I wasn't really prepared for it.

"Why the fuck do you have our son spending time with Sean? That nigga ain't his daddy. He got a daddy to do that with. I take care of him, I give him money every month and I am physically there. I ain't no bum ass nigga."

"Really, Randall? We all know you're an amazing father, and you know over the past few years Sean and I always had outings with Cam and his mentees. Camden only knew him as a friend. Now that Sean and I have moved forward into a relationship you want to complain? Why you weren't trippin before?"

"Look, Chelsea, I hear you but I'm not feeling no other nigga hanging with my son, PERIOD! I don't care if I ain't trip before because I am now. I just need you to respect that."

"Sean isn't an ordinary dude to me or Cam. He has always been a great friend and he treats Cam good. I am not going to make this into a big deal! I'll make sure we don't do anything inappropriate around him but Sean not being around isn't gonna happen." There was a long pause after my statement and then Randall hung up.

Walking into my condo's lobby I was hesitant. I felt there was a chance Randall would be there. I hadn't told him where I lived, but Randall had his ways of finding out.

"I figured I'd come in person to talk to you since you couldn't understand me over the phone. Was there bad reception or something?" Randall shouted in my face as I walked towards my door.

I was pissed off. "What do you want now, damn? Stop popping up unannounced. Shit, I didn't even tell you where I lived."

"I'll follow your rules when you follow mine. Why you gotta be like that and be with a man in front of my kid?"

I continued to open my door and replied, "I moved on Randall. And that comes with the territory. You moved on from me too a long time ago, remember?"

He walked inside and kept fussing. He was belligerent which was different. He held me up on the wall, "Listen to what the fuck I'm saying. I do not want him around my son! I am the only man Cam needs in his life and if I have to go to Sean I will. I ain't no pussy and you know that shit."

I shoved him off me. He stumbled backward but caught himself. There was rage in his eyes that made me alarmed, thinking he would flip out at any moment. Luckily, that didn't transpire. Instead, he paced around the dining room table then towards the living room. He eventually calmed himself down and sat on my couch with his elbows propped on his knees and hands rubbing his head. I knew something seemed different with him but I couldn't figure it out. I walked passed him and realized he was drunk. He did slur quite a bit and his breath smelled like straight liquor.

"Are you stupid? You say you're a great dad but you're sloppy ass drunk and you drove over here? Cam can't do nothing with you behind bars, or better yet dead. What the fuck are you thinking? Can you imagine how that would look with you getting a DUI? I need you to get your shit together and get the fuck out of my place!"

I went into my room to shower and when I returned he had fallen asleep on my couch. I tried to wake him up and tell him to leave but he was knocked out cold. He was drunk to the point of no return.

His phone rung and I looked at it as it lit up, "Basketball Coach." I decided to let him sleep it off but was hoping that would be the end of it.

I woke up to something rubbing my thighs. It was dark and I completely forgot I had company a few hours back; 4:30 am my clock read.

I looked down and Randall prowled in between my legs. "What the fuck man?" I yelled. He seemed unbothered as he moved his hands up my satin night dress.

"Damn I miss touching you girl. If you would only give me one more chance." I pulled away but he grabbed me and got on top.

"Randall, if you don't get your trifling hands off me, I'mma fuck you up. And you know I'm not playing." He studied my eyes, though hesitant, he got off.

"So, we're really over huh?" His eyes were watery but I knew not to invite him.

"Get the fuck out Randall, I respect you as the father of our son, but that is it. You have always been good to both Cam and me and I'm not sure where this is coming from, but you have ruined any chance of us ever being friends. Please leave me alone."

He backed away with his hands up, "Ok, I'mma do that."

He walked out of my room and I followed him until he walked out the front door. I locked it behind me and fell to the floor tearful. I was upset, I didn't want to be rude to him but he was trippin' and out of bounds. I heard my phone chant a melody signaling Sean's call but I was too distraught to bother him with my problems.

When I finally got into the bed, I contemplated on telling Sean but decided against it. But I did return his call.

"Hey, babe!" Sean shouted like it wasn't early as hell on my end.

"Hey."

"I was thinking maybe you can fly down to Miami and invite your friends since I will be there touring in four days. I wanted to do an intimate gathering on a yacht with you."

"That sounds great, I'll make that happen."

"I can't wait to taste you again Chels. Shoot, my dick stiff now thinking about it."

"I don't believe you, let me see." Sure enough, Sean propped the phone up and there his dick stood long and strong and I was hotter than a log burning fire.

There was no way I'd miss going to Miami. I went from not getting no action to receiving it whenever I'd please. I needed that time away since I had drama here in my personal life with Randall.

Miami consisted of nothing but sunny skies and a good time.

The wind blew my hair freely while my girls and I danced away on the yacht.

Earth Wind and Fire blasted as Sean came near us singing, ♪♫ *"Dancing in September.* Y'all don't know nothing about that. This what my parents used to play."

Sean was happy and his boys were behind him singing along. Our group of friends was the embodiment of a great time. I found myself being more spontaneous and carefree when in their company. We were a group of sixteen and everyone seemed to be coupled up in some way.

A while later, I spotted Riana doing a striptease for her boo Santos. She kept their relationship under wraps because she wasn't sure where they were headed, but now they were serious and she didn't mind letting the world know.

Benji, on the other hand, had one of his female friends onboard. No one knew much about Ri and his doings besides Sean and me, but I could tell Benji was bothered by her actions with Santos. I could only hope this outing ended with both of them being happy.

We had been on the boat for about two hours as the sun descended down. We finally settled down to eat some food. "You all so lame, why ain't nobody drinking these drinks? What y'all scared of?" Benji questioned while holding a bottle of Hennessy.

"Hell, we want to make it off this yacht and not drown to death," Shooter fussed.

After a while, the girls and I were ready to go for a swim. As the yacht came to a halt, we leaped out one by one. I ended up on Sean's neck while Ri was on Santos. We enjoyed some pleasurable time by playing a few games. We even beat the guys in a few races, though they claim they let us win. The trip couldn't get any better.

I could tell everyone was getting restless considering we did an excursion with Dolphins earlier that day. One thing I knew for sure, our bodies would pay for the longing and suffering.

As it got darker, the boat illuminated with blue and purple lights. The stunning glow brought comfort. We played a few more games on the deck and later went to the club.

It was jam-packed but the guys rented out a private section so we could enjoy ourselves. My girls were on their worst behavior. From what I saw, they should have gone back to the room. Ri was grinding and fucking Santos, no exaggeration. Benji seemed fully immersed in my homegirl San, despite his other friend being there. They seemed inseparable through the nightfall and the electrifying energy that ran through them made its way to Sean and me.

Sean's deep, sensual voice awakened my senses, "Can I have this dance?" While extending his hands to me, he pulled me close and held me tight as we danced to Ed Sheeran's 🎵 "Thinking Out Loud." It felt so good for us to sing and dance to this since I loved the song anyways. It was actually funny to see such a sensitive side to Sean.

My phone buzzed like crazy and after taking a look at it I noticed several tags that featured me. There were people in the club recording us live. I watched our every move simultaneously via Instagram. I showed Sean and he cackled. It didn't bother us, it was nice to know we were no longer worried about what others thought.

After the dance, Sean and I talked about our plans and our future since he was nearing the end of his tour. He felt we had known each other for quite some time and thought it wouldn't hurt to try living together. I expressed that maybe we were moving too fast but he didn't see the big deal since we were always together anyway.

"What about Cam? Don't you think it may seem weird for him?"

"Not really. We've spent more than enough time together for him to be comfortable with me"

"I guess we'll see but it's not a definite, ok?" Sean didn't answer but instead licked his lips and gave me a seductive look.

I walked to a more private area of the club while Sean trailed behind me. The deserted area was very dark with a big, round purple velour chair that Sean decided to sit on. I had on a short black dress which Sean enjoyed. I was unaware when he unzipped his pants. I just knew that in seconds, I was in his lap. He carefully slipped his fingers inside my wetness, simultaneously gliding my panties to the side. His hardness slithered in and made its attack.

If someone were to come up, I don't think they would have been able to tell what was happening since I was sitting directly on top, not facing him. He shifted, pushing his hips up gradually, not wanting to be noticed.

Slowly I moved my hips on top, putting a little umph on him. Sean licked my ear whispering, "Damn baby I don't have no rubber with me." He acted as if he was concerned but obviously didn't care since he was already in there.

"It's ok, I have an IUD anyways."

Sean continued to fill my creampie and I was only a few more strokes away from giving him all my icing.

He stopped me in my tracks, grabbed my hands and moved me towards a spot further in the back of the club. In front of a banister, he overpowered my core from the back. The rush of not getting caught was high and I loved it. Moments later we reached our peak.

That night, I made a vow to keep a condom with me at all times. I wanted to always be safe. Sean and I were tested a few months back, and part of our thing as friends was to be tested together. Since, Sean knew we were safe, he concluded we could stop using them once he ran out of the pack. I argued against it for a while but eventually dismissed the idea since I was on some form of birth control.

CHAPTER TEN

SEAN

SITTING courtside seats with a group of my boys and Benji, I observed the jam-packed basketball game. Tonight, Los Angeles played against Miami. This was my last day in Miami until I would head to Louisiana for the rest of my stateside tour.

This time in Miami went smooth since I was working and still having fun. I felt a bit hungover from the previous night on the yacht. I barely got any rest and was running off of four hours of sleep. I checked my phone to make sure Chelsea and her friends made it back to LA and to my surprise, I had several texts from her.

Hey, letting you know I'm home.

I meant to talk to you about something but wanted to wait until you're free.

Call me after the game and let me know you made it to your room safe.

I love you.

I responded to her texts, *I'm glad you're home and yeah I'm at the game but I'll definitely call you as soon as it's over. I LOVE YOU* 😘

Seconds later, *I love you too.* 💋

During halftime, fans swarmed my way for autographs but I was in no mood for that. I wanted to chill. I did sign a few things and made my way to the restroom when I saw a girl I recognized. "Hey Sean, how have you been?" I stood face-to-face with my ex whom I was crazy over back in the day but I cheated and you know where that went.

"Hey Courtney, I'm alright, it's good seeing you." I couldn't help to size her up, she was still fine with those big ass titties. But I knew I wouldn't go there. We talked a little while longer about our families before saying our goodbyes. Walking back towards the door, "Hey Sean, in case you need anything while in Miami you can call me you know." I didn't respond.

I did my usual, talked shit and enjoyed the game. "Aye man am I trippin' or is Randall looking at you funny?" Benji questioned. If he was I couldn't understand why because I rooted for the team he was playing for. I could care less who had the ball, I just wanted them to win.

"Randall Neal with the steal and down the court he goes... Oh, oh, oh, he goes for the three and swish, it's in!" The commentator went on as the crowd rumbled.

The game was now 96 to 92, with LA in the lead. This had been a close game all night and everyone sat at the edge of their seats. After Benji pointed out Randall's behavior, I too noticed him. He stared at me with a nasty look on his face. I wasn't sure why since he was no longer with Chelsea. He just saw me at her condo in Atlanta a few months back and didn't say nothing bad about it. I let the thought drift out of my mind, maybe we was trippin.

The game ended, 110 to 100 and LA won. It was great to see a lot of wins for LA. So far they were undefeated. My boys talked about going out to a party while I told them I would go back to my room. No more than a minute into the conversation with them, I saw Randall making his way to me.

"Let me holla at you real quick," Randall motioned while wrapping his arms around my neck. I noticed my boys and Benji looking at us crazy but I told them I'd be back. We walked out back to a secluded area that had a big sign that read **Authorized Personnel Only**. Moments later Randall started talking.

"No disrespect but I'm feeling funny about you being around Camden. And it's not that you're with Chelsea that bothers me but I don't want Cam to start looking at you as a father figure since I'm in his life." I couldn't be mad at his feelings but I had my own take on things too.

"Randall, man-to-man, I would never do anything to disrespect you but I do care about Cam. Honestly, over these past few years I've grown close to him and he always knew I was more of a friend to Chelsea's an——"

Randall cut me off and got a bit louder, "Nah, I talked to Cam the other day and I asked him what he'd been up too and he talked a lot of good stuff. Then he mentions having a great game night with you and Chelsea and he fell asleep watching a movie with the two of you. That shit got my blood boiling so I knew I needed to come to you."

"Yeah, that happened but what's the big deal? Me and Chels are together now so I do plan to make him comfortable with me. It's not like I will have him calling me daddy or anything. Shit, I ain't gon tell him to do anything. I want him to be himself and do whatever he feels."

I caught myself walking into his face, "Be happy I'm not no fuck ass nigga out here disrespecting your son or the mother of your kid."

Out the corner of my eyes, I saw his teammates walking towards us. Randall was being extra with the hand movements and his tone. I wasn't about to let dude disrespect me, I was gon hold mines and he had to deal with wherever this went.

"I tell you what, next time I hear you been around Cam, you gon see about me."

"Nigga fuck you, I do what the fuck I want!" Before I could keep going Benji was in front of us making sure things didn't go further. The crowd around us recorded the incident and my thoughts were on Cam seeing this but I was in too much rage.

"Yeah, do that and see what the fuck happens. Oh—I bet you didn't know I spent the night at your girl's house either huh? Yeah, that night I realized just how much I missed feeling on her. So, keep talking shit and I'mma have to get her back. If you know what's best, you would keep dating her and leave my son out of it. Believe me, I can have her back. Why you think she didn't kick me out of her place the other night?"

I was fueled, my adrenaline afforded me to push Benji out the way and my fist went straight into Randall's jaw. Randall fell back and within seconds his fist caught my cheeks slightly but I avoided the hard hit. We fought with every hit landing on its target. The team wasn't able to hold us back much.

Benji was the onsite type of guy and I noticed his hand getting ready to swing at Randall. "Benji, I got it, let me handle mine," I shouted. But someone else intervened. "Get the fuck back, get the fuck back," an officer shouted. This Suge Knight look-a-like grabbed me and practically yoked me up. Randall's teammates finally got a hold of him.

Despite being held up by the man, I continued voicing how I felt, "Since you claim you can get Chelsea, go be with her. At the end of the day, I'm good with or without her. But remember, as long as I'm with her, I got Cam too. I can't love her and not love him. If what you're saying is true and you've been sleeping over there then you can have it all. I ain't about to be fighting over nobody."

"Oh, nigga it's true. I stayed over her place and she didn't mind. If you know like I know then you know women gon do what they want."

My hands were tense, I was so hurt emotionally that I could barely focus. This nigga says he spent the night but why hadn't she told me that? I didn't understand what she could have been hiding. My mind spun in a whirlwind, I needed to leave ASAP.

"Listen, Sean, it's obvious both you and Randall are pissed off and I don't know none of you personally. What I do know is that this doesn't look good. All these people are recording, so I need you to just leave. I don't want to arrest you or Randall but I got a job I need to keep. So get out of here and stay out of trouble," the officer pleaded.

Not even an hour later, I had thousands of notifications from being tagged in the altercation. My anger transpired to another level so I decided to go out with the boys. Chelsea called over a hundred times and I ignored each and every one. Fuck her and whatever she had going on. I felt she made a fool of me. If Randall was honest then there's no reason for me to not know why he had to spend the night. I needed to know if he was telling the truth so I went to text her, only she beat me to the punch.

Babe, it's not what it seems. Randall is lying!

Me: **Did Randall spend the night at your house, YES or NO?**

A few minutes later she replied, **Yes, but not like he said. I tried to get him to get out—** All I needed to see were the words, yes and I immediately stopped reading. "Fuck her!"

I stared at several naked women, they danced and tried to get my attention. "Come on man, you wanna get a private dance with ole girl?" My brother tried to convince me to enjoy and do me. I shook my head no and continued drinking my Ciroc. I took shots back to back, I needed to forget everything that happened.

I noticed a few basketball players, actors, and musicians in the club but stayed to myself. Then I saw my ex. How could I see her at the game and ironically in the same club, in the same night? "Wow, I can't believe I ran into you again. Mind if I join you?" I didn't respond but listened to her talk about not being stressed and living my best life. Then she started rubbing my knees and slowly moving her hand up my thighs. My pants immediately held a huge bulge. I did have a thought in my mind to stop her but I didn't. "Let's get out of here," she whispered in my ears.

I sat in the dim private room watching her. She wasn't a dancer at the club but she decided to perform for me anyways. She undressed quickly, tossing her bra off and some part of me wanted her. I remembered the good times we shared. She was a freaky girl that I knew would do anything and everything if I said the word.

She sat in front of me, moving her panties to the side as I watched her play with herself. I wanted her bad as fuck. "I know you miss this Sean?" She said erotically. Without having a chance to answer, she came closer and got on her knees while unbuckling my pants. Seconds later she faced my dick.

What the fuck was I doing? I knew this wasn't right but my mind told me to fuck everything. "Courtney, damn you turning me on but——."

"I want you, Sean"

"Yeah, but let's stop, I don't feel right. Get dressed and we can go back downstairs."

She looked at me with rage and confusion.

"Ok, are you sure?"

"Yes."

The old me would have let her give me head, jack me off or better yet fuck. But I couldn't do it. By the time her shirt was on, a knock crept at the door. "Who the hell would come up to a private room, I had security at the front?" I thought out loud.

"Excuse me sir but Lexi is demanding to see you and—."

Lexi came barging in, cutting security off.

"Damn, you move on quick. Oh, and helllooo Courtney!! Why you looking like that girl, you don't remember me? You and I had a threesome with Sean." I was confused at how this Lexi bitch kept popping up everywhere I go.

"What the fuck are you doing here? Damn, do you not understand I don't like you?"

"No, what I do understand is I need to come clean to you about something and I don't think Courtney needs to hear this."

"Lexi don't fuck with me, what?"

"I want you to know I'm pregnant and I know it's yours because my cycle hasn't been on since I fucked you three months ago."

"Are you stupid? It's been more than 3-months since I fucked you. I know this because it was a week before the basketball playoffs and now the season has started over. Plus, I used protection with you and I'm sure nothing busted. Who the fuck you think you fooling? If you don't get your lyin' ass up out of here, it's gone be a problem!"

Lexi started crying, "Are you sure about that? I always keep up with what and who I do, and I know it's been three months."

"I don't care what you think. I know for a fact it's been six months and if I was you I would try to figure who to pin this baby on, because it won't be me."

Courtney stood baffled, she stared at me with disbelief but said nothing. I felt stressed and needed to get the hell up out of there. I found Benji with the boys and told them what was going on. "Damn boy, your night all fucked up. Your girl might be cheating and now another woman claims she carrying your baby. What the fuck you got going on?" Dion yelled.

"Nothing! I know for a fact Lexi not pregnant with my kid, it's been months and I used a rubber. Not only that, if she was pregnant from a few months ago her stomach would show something. Look at her when she comes out, her whole stomach out with no pudge."

"I saw her and she has no sign of pregnancy. She might be pregnant but she in her early stages," Dion agreed.

"But I don't know what to think with Chelsea. She has always been real with me and the whole Randall situation is messing up my head. I wanna sit and talk to her but damn.... Now, this whole Lexi shit is gon hit the blogs because she always does shit to get attention." My boys looked at me shaking their head.

By the time I got in the car, my driver looked back and

told me what he was hearing about the whole Randall situation. I knew shit was bad when the driver started talking to me. He never got in my business, but I knew I was looking and feeling like shit. The blow really hit when I got a text from Chelsea.

Hey, I know you're mad and I'll accept that. But you should have listened to me and heard the truth before you decided to have sex with your ex Courtney at the club tonight. After she sent that text, she sent me a video from Instagram with me and Courtney headed to the private room. The worse part was seeing Courtney's hands grabbing my belt buckle in the video.

For the record, I never messed with Randall, he came to my house drunk and yelling about Cam. When I tried to get him out, I couldn't. I did kick him out eventually and I have footage to prove that since my hallway has cameras. But there's no need for that now since all it takes is a rumor for you to cheat on me. Tonight, you proved to me that you are no different than Randall and you don't know how to be faithful. And before I forget, congratulations on you and Lexi baby! Don't bother replying or calling, I'm already blocking your number after I send this.

I felt a knot in my chest as tears welled in my eyes. Seconds later another video came thru of Lexi showing her ultrasound picture and confirming her pregnancy with a caption, 'Yay, I'm so happy to announce Sean B and I are having a baby!'

"FUCK!" I screamed as I threw my phone down. I couldn't take much more. I knew for a fact this wasn't my baby but I knew no one would believe that until the baby came. Then to think I was stupid enough to go into a private room with my ex.

I did try to call Chelsea. Her phone went straight to voicemail and my text was never delivered. I had to figure a way to stay focused until I could see her again. Til then I needed to breathe and say fuck the world.

CHAPTER ELEVEN

CHELSEA

"I THINK it's absolutely insane that Chelsea and Sean are both cheating on each other so early on in their relationship. We don't need more evidence than what we have seen this weekend," a youthful blonde lady guffawed on the TMI show.

"Lexi always claims to be pregnant by some high-profile man, how can we be sure that she is indeed messing with Sean?"

I had to exit out of the TMI app on my phone because obviously, we were out here looking like some damn fools. I tried to sleep my days away but I couldn't help to think how stupid I had been for giving Sean a chance. I knew what he was capable of but I took the risk anyway.

I went over to the mirror to reflect, and there I stood with bags under my eyes. I was feeling defeated. I hadn't felt this way since the whole incident with Randall cheating. How could I have been so naive?

Tears were pouring as my phone rang. My eyes were so full, I couldn't read who was calling. I answered, "YES?"

"Are you crazy? Don't talk to me like that. You think you can talk to me how you want, now that you're gaining some success and accolades?" My mom fussed but yet made me smile.

"Sorry ma, I didn't know it was you."

"I know what the media is saying and I am not here to fuss. What I do know is that you are not who they say you are. I know you didn't cheat on Sean, but I can't say the same for him." My heart sunk to my stomach. I didn't want to hear that.

"Yeah, I know mom. But I can't believe Randall made it seem like that. I never wanted him in the house and I did kick him out eventually," I broke down crying. I told my mom the whole story.

"You should have told Sean about it, had you done that it wouldn't have been a surprise and things could've gone differently. Have you tried talking to him?"

I remained quiet for a while but explained that too. "How can I ever talk to Sean again when Lexi is supposed to be pregnant? What about the videos of his ex walking him into a private room in the club? There is no coming back from that."

"Yeah but as you know now, what seems to be one thing may not really be that. You two need to sit down and talk about it and come up with a conclusion. Don't let these nobodies make a fool of the both of y'all. Take it from me, did you forget who I'm married too? My relationship with your dad wasn't easy at first. Being married to a prize fighting boxer presented its challenges. A lot of times the rumors were just that and there was no truth in it. So, find out and stop moping around. And take a damn shower. I can already imagine what you over there looking like. I bet you got bags under your eyes too, huh?"

"Ok mom, I'll talk to you later, love you!" I hung up the phone. I knew she was right but I needed to figure out my next move. I had several speaking engagements and needed to find a way to brief myself on the upcoming events. I wanted to be able to talk and be confident in all I was going to say.

"About time you called me back. I was so worried about you," Ri said on the other end of the phone. She went on to fill me in on everything that was going on in the outside world and she advised me on how I should go about everything. I needed a way to see Sean in person but I wasn't ready to unblock his call either. As childish as that may have sounded, I didn't want to let him off the hook yet. He still needed to understand where I was coming from.

"Oh, I talked to Sean too Chelsea." My heart crushed into my chest at the thought.

"He says the videos weren't how it seemed. I listened to his story but I cussed his ass clean out for you too. I told that nigga he wasn't shit and I hoped he choke and die." Me and Ri laughed instantaneously.

"But you know what's funny? As soon as I told him how dirty he was for cheating, he turned around and told me he learned from the best, which was me since I fucked Benji and Santos."

I busted out into laughter. As mad as I was I knew he would be the one to talk shit.

"But wait a minute, he can't afford to joke right now. I'mma have to really look into this, I really don't want to leave him but I don't want to look dumb."

Riana kept hyping me up and now I was ready to find out the truth.

I got myself together as I entered the elevator to the 7th floor of NRW Studios. I was due to have an interview about an upcoming project that was soon hitting theaters. I looked better than I felt. I had on a one-piece black and pink Dior bodysuit. To brighten my day, I added pink pumps and some matching earrings. I was flawless indeed and I wanted them to see that regardless of what went down.

"Chelsea, oh my," the man said while taking a second look at me. "You don't look down at all, after all these allegations, one would think you would look and feel horrible." I smirked at his comment and greeted him. I sat in the chair and noticed they were setting up the cameras for the interview.

"Is there anything off limits before we start?" I thought about it then replied, "Not necessarily but I don't want to go into details about me and Sean." The man and his co-host looked at each other but didn't complain.

"Welcome back to NRW, where we bring you all the entertainment and real news. Today we have Chelsea with us and isn't she just fabulous?" The lady asked her co-host.

"Heck yeah, she is!" He replied.

"So, Chelsea tell us about your upcoming project with Dorien?"

"This one is full of action but yet very emotional. As you all know he takes a lot of losses in this film. But the comeback is crazy and I play his looney girlfriend."

"Yes, the trailer shows you guys getting pretty close, was that true in reality too? Did this bring you two closer together and do y'all hang out now?"

"I have gotten to know him and he is amazing to hang with, but we're just cool. He is fun to work with."

"Is there anything you would like to address with all the rumors with NBA player Randall? We know he accused you of being with him—." I stopped him in his tracks.

"Sorry to cut you off but he never said he was with me in that way. Yes, he stopped by but he came to fuss and I had him leave a while after. I haven't been with my son's father since my college days if you want to go there."

Both hosts were shocked at my honesty but they respected it.

"Oh, sorry. We didn't mean to offend you but we were trying to give you a chance to clarify. As there has been so much speculation about you and Sean breaking up."

"Well there's always rumors but not all things are true," I said while batting my eyes and smiling. I wasn't going to validate their thoughts on where Sean and I were with our relationship.

"Well you heard it from us first, Chelsea has done no wrong and we hope her and Sean can see things through. Also, go check out her new film, *Nightmare on Hurst.*"

As soon as we were done taping, I had so many notifications hitting my phone. Since this was a live show, people were already on alert to my remarks.

"*I can't believe Randall made it seem like he hit that again.*"

"*I don't know why Randall can't move on.*"

"*I don't believe Chelsea, she knows he tapped that again.*"

"*Even if Chelsea is honest, Sean still has a baby on the way with Lexi.*"

After that comment, I had to put the phone down. I needed a breather but then I got a direct message from Sean.

"PLEASE READ... I NEVER CHEATED! I SWEAR I DIDN'T! I know you blocked me because I keep calling and it's going to voicemail. But give me a chance to tell you the truth. I'm sorry I didn't give you a chance to explain but I was hurt. I haven't been able to do anything. I can't even focus on my shows. Please don't leave me hanging like this Chels. And Lexi is lying about me being the father too. I know for a fact it's not mine. Just call me."

My heart ached to read the message but how does he know it's not his? He has had sex with her but last time I checked we got tested a month after they had sex, which wouldn't add up.

Another video surfaced but this time he was doing the talking as the paparazzi cornered the camera in his face. "Is it true that Lexi is pregnant with your baby?"

He looked up with anger in his eyes, "Does it look like I would be stupid enough to have unprotected sex with a hoe that's been passed around? Hell no, I ain't the daddy. I haven't messed with that girl in over six months. So, she needs to pin the baby on whoever she's been fucking!" Then he pushed the camera out of his face as he got into his car.

Hearing that made me realize if he is being truthful then the dates match mine and Lexi couldn't be pregnant with his kid. She should at least be five to six months pregnant.

"Hey girl, I found out some more information. Lexi is actually at Studio Twelve if you want to pop up on her. You know I got the latest 411 and I need you to check that hoe. I kind of don't believe her. But-I-gotta-get-back-to-work. Let me know what happens." Riana was always the detective in the crew and she always knew where to go and I sure as hell appreciated her call to catch me up.

An hour later I pulled up to Studio Twelve. I prayed things would go smooth but I also knew the type of person she was. As I got closer I could hear her big ass mouth through the double doors. I walked in without knocking, causing Lexi and the two engineers to look at me in shock. No one saw me coming but I didn't care.

"Oh, you came to find out about my baby daddy?" Lexi said sarcastically. I went into the booth and snatched the headphones off her ear. She was shocked but didn't do a thing but fuss.

"Don't you put your hands on me," she yelled.

"Look, I didn't come here to fight you or cause a scene. But I did want to know what really happened between you and Sean? And if you truly thought this baby was his?"

She rolled her eyes and stepped out the booth. "Yes, me and him have been having sex. We fucked after you left the album release party." My nose flared as anger filled me. "I don't believe you," I said with an attitude.

"Well don't. I'm just stating facts and besides I was already pregnant before that anyways. He gets attitudes with me because he feels like I am all on him but the truth is, he is always calling me for booty calls and since I like him a lot, I give in. Just like the other night in the club, his ex was fucking him and she obviously gave in too, like me. Who would turn away that big dick of his? Then his head game is a killer, I'm sure you know about that?"

"Bitch! Yes, I know what his dick and mouth are like but he told me he never put his mouth on you in that way but I guess that's irrelevant now. I will be straightforward with you, me and him have always had a close relationship. I don't see why he would lie about what y'all have done since we weren't together at the time anyway. Why lie about that when he told me about the threesome you two had with his ex, Courtney?" Her eyebrows started scrunching together as she heard me make these revelations.

"Yeah, I know about the time he fucked you and then Dion messed with you not too long after. What about you fucking ole' dude over there, remember who caught you? Dion did and that same night you called Sean crying because you thought that would make things worse for you and him. Girl, he never liked you like that, he was just having a good time. Last time I checked you haven't messed with him since the day you cried about me spending the night at his house. That's the night he left you at the hotel, remember? And for the record, I was never fucking him then, but I did convince him to get checked a few weeks later. I already knew I was catching feelings so I took the proper precautions with our STD screenings because I knew if I made love to him, I didn't want to worry since you too were so scandalous. But you aren't the problem, he is. He should know better than to stick his dick in any ole thing. I know you knew you weren't the only one he was messing with? But as I check myself, I ask, am I the only one? But something tells me I am. And I believe that.

So, if you think you and this maybe baby is going to fuck us up, you got another thing coming. If you are telling the truth and this baby is his, you can have him."

After my long speech, I walked out of the booth and studio. My heart ached at the fact that he could have gotten her pregnant but that still would have happened before us hooking up which wasn't as bad. Unfortunately, I knew I couldn't be with him if the results proved it to be true. To think he cheated on me with his ex was another issue. At this point, I was livid and could only pray to find reprieve from my problems.

CHAPTER TWELVE

SEAN

THE FOLLOWING days had been pure hell. Chelsea and I were on every entertainment blog and I even caught a glimpse of the local news station reporting on us. I was hoping to be back in Chelsea's good graces soon, but everything being said about me kept leading back to cheating allegations and becoming a father. I tried to keep it together during my shows but I couldn't.

There was a particular song that I wrote about Chelsea before we made it official and that did it. While performing, the crowd sung along but before the second verse my eyes welled up. I was emotional, barely making it through, but I regained my composure and finished with a bang. That didn't matter, the video made its rounds and people had a lot to say.

"Why he pouting over a female?"

"He should have been faithful!"

"I bet he learns his lesson now!"

"He needs to learn to keep his dick in his pants."

Those were some of the reasons I did not do relationships. I despised the fact that everyone assumed things. Nothing was private.

"Bruh? Did you hear anything I said? You have been sitting here quiet for at least five minutes. Come on man, eat your food," Benji screeched in my ears. We were a few hours from flying out to St. Louis so we decided to grab a bite to eat while watching the NBA Playoffs.

"My bad man, I have so much on my mind. I wish shit wasn't like this. How the hell I even get into this shit? First Randall, then my dumb ass walked into a room with Courtney in public and then Lexi. I ain't even cheat on Chelsea bruh. Do you know I stopped Courtney? I told her I ain't feel right."

Benji pushed his chair back and his eyes grew big, "Damn, so you ain't fuck or get your dick sucked? I was gon ask you the night of, but I knew you were upset."

"No, I ain't did shit. A nigga got hard but that was it."

Benji stared and smiled. "Well, you ain't did shit then! Go get your girl back. If your dick ain't go in her then what the fuck?"

"Those videos say otherwise, you know Chelsea was already scared to be with me because of Randall's cheating ass."

Our conversation got interrupted by Timothy. He was a big-time producer that made hit after hit. "My boys," he shouted while dapping us up and pulling a chair up to talk. "So, you in the dog house huh?"

I gave a fake smile. "Dang man, that's the first thing you say after not seeing me in months?"

"Nah, but I have some info that I think you would want to know."

Benji and I eyed each other while pulling our seats up, not wanting to miss a beat. Then I asked, "What is it, I been getting all types of bad news and hopefully this will be positive?"

"Not being nosey, but has it been at least three months since you messed with Lexi?"

I looked at him confused, I didn't know where he was coming from. "Hell, it's been way longer than that. It's been at least six months."

"That's great, I can tell you that you aren't the father. Lexi is only eight weeks pregnant and I know this because my boi Pete believes he's the father. But he doesn't want anyone to know. See, I came in here to pick up an order and was happy to see you sitting with your brother. As you may already know, Pete has been with Lexi a lot over the past few months but they got into it once he saw all the messages she sent you.

He said he could tell you weren't interested in her by all your responses. But what he didn't understand was why she still chased you after your text messages specifically said to leave you alone?"

"Wow, she never mentioned Pete but hell I never gave her a chance. I been trying to dodge her. I guess you are right, this is good information to know but she seems to want to run with me being the father. I feel like things will stay the same until I take a DNA test. I'm willing to take a test because I know Chelsea will want me to if I want to be with her. Man, I appreciate you coming to me about this."

"I got you... But I hope my boi Pete drop her completely, regardless if he's the dad or not. She obviously for everybody."

"Yeah, I learned that early on with her, but it was all fun and games, nothing serious."

"Let me get my food before it gets cold. If you need me you know my number." I was glad to hear that from him but I knew I still needed a game plan to convince Chelsea.

We watched Tim walk away, as he disappeared Benji couldn't wait to express his thoughts. "I believe him but I also think his boy Pete wanna know if you were still fucking his bitch. What you think?"

"Yeah, that thought ran across my mind too. I'm just glad to know she's very early in her pregnancy. I know I strapped up, but if she was six months pregnant I would be paranoid."

"Right, that was good info. I guess we should celebrate and get some drinks. We should toast to not being the father!"

I shrugged and contemplated my next move. I knew things would clear up but also remembered that I had an interview coming up that Chelsea was a part of. But I wasn't too sure she would actually show up. But just in case she did, I planned to set the record straight.

Peering into the crowd, I noticed just how much love and support I had. After all the allegations people were yelling,

"We believe you, Sean," while others screamed out how much they loved me.

As the crowd kept going, Sheryl the host, had to remind them that we were live and recording. "Ok ladies and gentlemen let's settle down. Sean, before the break you gave out scholarships to three lucky students. That was an amazing gift in itself; but what other advice can you give that you feel would benefit them for the rest of their life?"

"There are so many things. Besides keeping God first, make sure you stay true to yourself and what you want. So often we're being influenced by the media and that really doesn't matter. When you hit rock bottom there's no one there but you. You have to get yourself up and go after your dreams.

Also, stop being lazy. You can have what you want if you work hard at it. Things don't just come to you, you gotta earn it, then take it. Even when it seems impossible, keep fighting. Everyday, do one thing to get closer to your dream. Eventually, it will be right there. Don't give up."

"Wow, you named some good ones. So, with all the turmoil in your life right now, are you saying you're going to get back up and try to fix things with Chelsea?"

"Hahaha, I knew that was coming but uh, yeah, I will do my best. I never cheated on her and I would elaborate but I think I owe it to her first, for us to speak privately. I want to make sure she's good."

"That's great because she's here. I know you two originally planned to do this together before all the drama. But since she still came I think it's safe to bring her on out." The crowd cheered as we waited for her appearance.

Chelsea walked out looking more stunning than ever. She wore some dark blue ankle fitting jeans with a blue and white fitted shirt that showed just a little bit of her breast. The white heels screamed FUCK ME and I was ready to jump every bone she had. Her glow made me think she hadn't missed me one bit. Chelsea sat on the other side of Sheryl, leaving me on the opposite end.

"Hi, Chelsea," Sheryl seemed enthusiastic.

"Hey, Sheryl," she returned while looking into the crowd, waving and blowing kisses since they were all yelling how much they loved her.

Her eyes met mine but she had no facial expression. Her expression went from blissful to obsolete. Her eyes were waterlogged but she stopped the tears from coming.

I spoke, breaking our awkward silence, "Hey Chelsea."

She dropped her head, seconds passed, she looked back up and took a deep breath, "Hey."

The crowd went ballistic.

"Is this the first time you two have seen and talked to each other since all the chaos?" Sheryl asked.

"Yeah, it is," I said with relief.

"Let's fix it here on the show. We're in the business of positivity and—."

Chelsea mouth took over and she shot the host a mean stare, "I don't know about all of that. There's a lot of personal stuff we need to take care of first." Then her head shifted my way, "Sean, these past few days have been horrible. I don't know where we're headed but I know together or not I need and want answers. So hopefully later we can actually..."

I was out my seat by the time she said hopefully. Near the end of her statement, I invaded her mouth. My tongue lashed inside, taking her breath away. She reciprocated the lust that burned inside of me.

The crowd cheered us on...

"How about we take a quick commercial break and we'll let these two catch up. When we come back, we'll see if there's a resolution."

We went to a private room in the back. Sheryl was such an amazing host, she brought out another guest to fill in for us until we got it together.

Once in the room, I drew Chelsea into my arms, holding her. She cried uncontrollably and I felt bad as hell.

"Baby it's ok, I promise things aren't the way it looked." I moved over to a chair and sat her in my lap.

"Listen, I didn't have sex with the girl in the video. I did go into the private room and I thought about messing with her. Only because I thought you had been with Randall."

She jumped into defense mode, "But I didn't even do anything with him!"

"Yeah, but you never said anything about that situation. I didn't even know he stayed at your place. All I know is what he said. But listen, as the girl started to undress, I told her to stop and go back out."

"Undress? Damn, all because you thought I did something. So, every time you get mad you gon go out, and do you?"

"No, I'm just telling you what happened that night. So, the girl got dressed and Lexi marched into the room. I hadn't talked or texted her and I still don't know how she knew where I was. Then she starts firing shots at me claiming she's pregnant with my baby. But I haven't had sex with her in six months, close to the beginning of basketball season."

"Hold on, let's back up, so how much clothes did she have off? Did she touch you or did you touch her?"

I was hesitant to answer, I felt uncomfortable since she was no longer the homie but more. "No, we didn't get that far. She told me to come upstairs with her and I followed. She started stripping, that's it."

Chelsea folded her arms and had a facial expression that could kill. "Mhm, whatever."

"Babe seriously, I didn't do anything with her. I can't believe I stopped myself either. In the past, I definitely would have done it, but that night I realized my love for you runs deep."

"Have you ever given Lexi head or kissed her?"

With raised brows, I shouted, "Hell nah! Come on Chelsea... I been telling you everything before and I would've admitted it now. I don't put my mouth on any and everything. I wanna believe you know me better than the way you're acting towards me."

I was a bit disturbed at the thought of her assuming or believing I did anything to Lexi other than fuck her. I knew the first time I messed with that girl I would be cautious and that never changed. Even with other girls I dealt with, I never opted to devour their insides. I was very skillful at giving head but I learned that over a period of time with only five women, despite having a lot of sexual partners.

"Anything else I need to know before I have to hear it from others?"

"No, but do you remember Pete, the one that..."

"I already know about that. I went to check Lexi in the studio the other day and the girl at the front desk already put me on game. I figured Lexi was bullshitting. But when the baby comes, I want you to take a DNA Test."

"Yeah, I figured you would say that. But I'll only do that as long as we can move forward in our relationship. I love you and I'm so sorry for allowing my actions to give any reason that I may be cheating."

She raised her head and kissed me. She gave me the most fervent kiss which reconfirmed where she wanted to be.

"Babe, I still wanna know what happened with Randall?" She procrastinated for a bit but then told me the story and anger filled me. Randall was doing the most but I knew I would eventually put him in his place.

A few minutes later we heard a knock, "Hey, you two are back up in ten minutes." I was happy to be on the same page but something was still missing.

I unfastened her pants, pulling them down to her ankles. "Bend over."

"Babe, we gon get caught. Don't you hear those footsteps passing by?"

Despite her pleading, her hands went down to the arm of the chair, as she obliged. My pants made their way down to my ankles and I whipped my dick out and plummeted inside her opening. My erection was welcomed by a firm grip of tightness and a cave that salivated excessively causing me to groan and sing her name. I was in ecstasy and understood why I hadn't cheated. I didn't feel the need to.

Her moans occupied the room as I pounded her backside. She shoved her ass closer to my bulk, allowing my dick to fill her. My body began to shudder and the intense feeling to explode inside her was at its height. Thrusting and gripping her waist, I leaned in to taste her. She was headed beyond her limits, "Sean, oohh, I'm 'bout to--!"

Retracting from our position, I faced her towards me, sitting her on a rectangular shaped table that filled a good bit of the room. I wanted to convey what I felt; the longing and passion I'd bottled up from not seeing her. So, I thrusted harder assaulting her spread. Her eyes rolled back, as she closed her lids, clawing my back. Finally, we reached satisfaction.

"We gave you a few extra minutes, hope you two lovebirds made up," a lady shouted. From the sound of it, I wouldn't be surprised if someone overheard us. I didn't care, I was glad to be back on track with my girl.

CHAPTER THIRTEEN

CHELSEA

♪♪ "I AIN'T NEVER GOING BACK, ayyee!" I rapped along with the crowd to Shooter's song. This song featured his sister Riana. LA was Ri's last stop on her tour. She was back home and I was happy to be supporting her and Shooter.

My clothes were drenched in sweat by the time the show was over, but I still snuck out, exiting thirty minutes before the end of the show in order to beat the crowd.

My optimistic mood extended beyond the clouds; Sean and I were in a better place. We both knew the truth but I still needed reassurance on the Lexi drama. Not to mention, I also happened to run into his ex, Courtney, who confirmed the exact story Sean gave. She apologized and I couldn't be mad. She wasn't my friend.

Walking down the hall out of the arena, I got a text from Sean, ***Letting you know I landed and I guess we can see each other whenever. It would be nice to see*** *you tonight.* My heart melted and instantly I felt a tingle below, which only meant she was ready. I swear my yoni had a mind of its own. I replied back, 🐱👀🍆.

I stuffed my phone back into my purse while looking for my car keys. Something wasn't right. I felt as if I wasn't alone. I turned around and observed my surroundings but I saw no one. I was only a few steps away from walking out the door when I heard, "Damn you leaving already?" I jumped at the sound of the voice, there Randall stood.

"Randall get the fuck out my face and leave me alone. You're so full of it."

"I'm sorry, Chelsea. I know I shouldn't have said what I did to Sean but I was pissed."

"Boy, you think I give two cents about your feelings? I used to care but now I don't give a flying fuck. I want you out of my life, but unfortunately, I know that's not possible." He stood in front of me and though he wasn't physically pinning me against the wall, he still had me stuck against it. He was so close to my face that the rest of his body remained no more than three centimeters away. I could feel his breath all on me.

"Can you just go?" I asked desperately while noticing tears rolling down his face. I could tell I hurt his feelings but that was no longer my concern.

"Yeah, I'll go but I do want to talk to Cam. So, make sure you have him call me. I been calling your parents but they never answer or return my calls."

"Mhm, I wonder why?" I said sarcastically.

"Look, I said I'm sorry. I mean that. But I'll holla at Sean, since it's obvious you love him and all. But you and I need to talk and stay in contact. I need to know about my son and I want and need to be there."

"You know I would never keep him away from you, hell you're his dad. Anyways, bye." I ended the conversation and slid away.

It was dark as I opened the door leading to my car. I could tell the concert ended since I saw a lot of people on the other side of the parking lot which read, "**PUBLIC**". There was a public parking and a friends and family one.

It was me and just a few other people in the family and friend's area, and before I made it to the car, I heard Shooter calling me. "Aye big head girl, wait on me." I turned around and smiled as he walked toward me. "You know you got a big ass head, don't you? Who else acknowledges such a name?"

I laughed at his joke and hit him upside his head.

"Shut the hell up! But damn, tonight was lit as hell. The brother and sister duo set the crowd on fire and personally, I don't know who else could pull off the shit y'all did?"

Shooter laughed and gave me the tightest hug. "Chelsea, thank you for supporting me and helping build my image. You've done so much for me when I was broke as hell and didn't have a dime to pay you. Even though I'm sure you did it since Ri is your best friend." He nudged me a laughed.

"But you are an amazing friend and I have this for you." I extended my hand as Shooter handed me an envelope. "I know I always paid you good once my money rolled in, but take this as a gift for the past when I didn't have anything to give you."

I glared into Shooter's eyes while squeezing his hand. I

valued our friendship but I never was the type to ask for something in return when I was doing out the kindness of my heart. When I opened the envelope, I saw a check for $50,000.

"Shooter no, I will not take that from you. Have you lost your mind? Save that money and invest it."

"Chill man, you did pro bono work for a whole year and do you remember it was you that helped me get to where I am? You showed me the ropes and even coached me on my speaking and etiquette for different occasions. After leaving home so young and not having a close relationship with my dad, I lacked many of the tools that you and your family gave me. That money is just a drop in the bucket for what I really owe you. I don't forget shit, you deserve it, so take it. PLEASE!"

After all that begging he did for me to keep the money, I took that shit and put it in my purse, locking it up in my trunk. He died laughing at my exaggeration. We talked for a while longer while I filled him in on the bull crap Randall was pulling.

"Shooter I'm telling you, I'm convinced Rand..." My statement couldn't be completed because my attention veered to my left where shots went off and within seconds, something cold hit my shoulder. What was cold instantly turned hot and the pain immediately intensified.

"Ugghh," I grunted while moving my palms to the wound. Shooter snatched me to the ground just as I felt another object puncture my flesh. I was confused, I barely could breathe and all I could hear was ringing in my ears. Shooter's face shifted out of focus. Now, I could only see a faint image of him and I could see a black car that resembled a suburban with three men hanging out the window. I was totally out of it, but I could feel tears streaming down my face. I knew something was wrong and it was confirmed when I couldn't even move.

Suddenly, I saw Ri looking hysterical with a heap of blood on her. She cried while holding me and for a second I assumed I was dead.

Maybe I was an apparition looking down at the action. The scene was so alive and real to me because after a while of not hearing anything, I eventually regained some audio. I heard Ri yell, "What the fuck man, what the fuck happened? Who the fuck did this shit?"

Shooter was devastated with his gun out. "I'mma kill em! They gon ride up like that? They knew she was standing by me. They could have waited. What the fuck man?" His hands were swaying back and forth. At the same time, he kept hitting his head with tears shooting down.

A crowd formed with countless amounts of cops and an ambulance eventually arrived.

"We have a young lady in her twenties that's about 5'4, weighing 125 lbs. She has a GSW to the left shoulder and a graze to her upper temporal area." After hearing those words from the paramedic everything went blank, pitch black.

I had to be in and out of consciousness, I kept hearing and

seeing bits and pieces. I knew I was in the Emergency Room but wasn't sure what all had happened. I saw the lights above me shining brightly through my semi-closed eyelids but I was also in full motion as several doctors transferred me from the gurney to a hospital bed.

"Ms. Collins, can you open your eyes?" The blonde lady asked me but I couldn't. My eyes were too heavy. "Can you wiggle your toes for me?" I tried, but failed.

"Ok, what are you going to do with her? Can she hear us? Is she even aware? Is she gonna live?" Ri was asking all sorts of questions.

Another lady with a deeper voice replied, "Please Riana, we are not sure of her current condition, but I assure you we will do all we can to make sure she recovers. We need to run some tests first and then we will know exactly what we're dealing with and how to proceed."

I can't recall how many hours went by before I finally heard, "Chelsea honey? It's Dr. Sarahano. You just had surgery and I want you to know that you are ok and in recovery. There's no need to try to respond or move, I know you're confused and we'll explain everything to you once you're alert and settled in your room."

I was nervous after hearing those words but I knew enough about the medical field to understand that this was there protocol regardless if my injuries were serious or not.

A sharp object was inserted through the left side of my upper arm and I felt an excruciating pain that radiated from my limbs to my fingers. Whatever shot they gave me, I knew it was for pain because within seconds I no longer felt the throbbing pain of my shoulder.

I wasn't sure how they knew I was hurting but I knew they were doing a good job watching me. Every so often I felt something cold touch my lips, which I assumed was ice. Then other times I felt someone wiping my face and talking to me.

The people who spoke to me would tell me what had happened and what to expect. I was at peace but felt a bit lonely. I couldn't tell how much time went by but I wondered where my family and friends were? I hadn't heard Ri's voice in a while and never had the strength to open my eyes.

"Ok, Chelsea, we gave you something that should help you be able to open your eyes. The lack of mobility you're feeling is due to the medication we have given you. Right now I'm going to shine a light at your eyes. Even if you can't open them, at least move your eyeballs or squeeze my hands. I need something from you," the doctor said with compassion.

"Umm, I hear you but I barely—," before getting all my words out, the doctor pressed the call button and stated, "Good job Chelsea. That's all I needed from you."

There was a team of medical professionals around me within minutes. Finally, I was able to open my eyes on my own. And in that instant, the medical team began taking my stats and examining me.

After one of the the doctors finished evaluating me he spoke, "Ms. Collins, I just want to inform you of exactly what's happening. First, in case you aren't aware, you have been shot. The bullet that was lodged in your shoulder has been removed. One bullet grazed you near your temple, causing only a laceration, so you were lucky. Had it hit you directly, you would be dead or depending where the bullet actually struck, you could've been in a vegetative state. When you were brought in, you were suffering from severe blood loss so we had to perform emergency surgery to stop the bleeding. From the looks of it, your body is responding well to treatment and if you continue to improve you should be able to go home in a week or so. You will need additional time to fully recover, but I see no problem with you doing so at home following the guidelines and directions we set forth. You will still need to come in for monitoring, so you won't totally be free from us."

Tears poured down my face as I took in all the words. My mind pondered on who and why would someone shoot at me? As my memory began to come back to that night, I do remember talking to Shooter and the list of enemies he has is longer than any track field.

After pondering, I asked one of the nurses to give me a mirror to observe myself. She was hesitant at first but she got up and left. I watched her walk away, noticing lots of flowers and 'Get Well Soon' balloons. I took a good look at my room. I had to admit, for a hospital, it was beautiful. I had floor to ceiling windows overlooking the city. Eyeing the bright sun beaming in gave me a sense of a new beginning.

The nurse returned. I took a careful look at my face. My caramel skin was intact but I did see where a gauze pad sat on the right side of my temple. As I looked further down I noticed my shoulders. Tugging at the blue and white gown I carefully inspected myself. There were several pads with blood stains seeping through it. Immediately I became queasy. I felt dizzy and light headed, and the nurse sensed my anxiety. She sat by me and wiped the tears that flowed.

I still felt beautiful but couldn't understand how this could be me. I did nothing wrong, I didn't knowingly have any enemies, who would want to hurt me? My mind raced until I fell fast asleep.

I kept having dreams of the moment before I ended in the hospital. Seeing Shooter and I talking and moments later Ri would cry out. As soon as I would wake up, I'd fall back asleep and repeat the pattern. I slept like crazy but I figured it was the medicine.

I forgot to ask the nurse how long I'd been in the hospital. Since I was able to open my eyes, I hadn't seen anyone. My feelings were all over the place until a knock disturbed my thoughts.

CHAPTER FOURTEEN

SEAN

I'D FINALLY TOUCHED BACK DOWN in LA. I finished my tour and was glad to know I would be in a place where I could give my full attention to Chelsea. I dropped an album a few months prior, finished an amazing tour and I was featured on everyone's song.

I explained all this to Benji as we exited the plane. As happy as Benji was with our talk, I noticed his focus remained on his phone. He was texting or browsing the web. But I wanted his full attention. "Damn nigga, I'm talking to you," I shouted at him.

He looked up startled, "My bad, there's something going on. I'm trying to see what's up." I was confused at his response but then our conversation got interrupted by his cell phone again. I knew someone had FaceTimed him but wasn't sure who. Benji walked away to answer it. He didn't say anything when he finished the call, and I noticed he was acting a bit weird.

His phone went off three times back to back. He ignored it. Then it went off again. "Damn who blowing you up?" I screeched.

With his head down, he whispered, "Riana."

I gave him a puzzled look as he explained he would talk to me once we were inside the truck. I didn't argue, maybe he was going through something with Riana?

Once inside the truck, my phone vibrated with hundreds of notifications but before I could pull the bar down on my iPhone, Benji stopped me. "Nah, I need to talk to you before you check your phone?"

"Oh, my bad. What's up? What you and Riana got going on?"

Benji's eyes were blank and this I knew was serious. "Sean, well um, something is wrong, very wrong and we have to go straight to the hospital."

My heart sped, I was nervous to hear why. I glared at him giving him a look of concern.

"Riana called to tell me she was at the hospital with Chelsea and she'd been shot."

I couldn't tell you what I did next, I was in a zone. When I did get it together, I was furious, punching the seats in the Denali truck.

"Bro, man chill, that ain't gon help, we headed there now, just calm down. Damn, you almost fucked me up with your jabs. She ain't dead man, she's in surgery as we speak."

I couldn't just sit there and talk to Benji, I needed a source at the hospital. I called Riana.

A weepy Riana answered, "Hey Sean, sorry I didn't call you first but I..."

"No, I don't care about that. Who and how did this happen? I texted her an hour ago and everything was fine."

"I don't know. I just know I came out and Shooter was screaming as I approached. She laid in his arms with blood everywhere. I don't remember anything else. I know the bullet was meant for Shooter. At least that's what he thinks."

"Fuck! Man, I just——— I just——," I couldn't finish talking. Benji grabbed the phone and finished talking to Riana.

I've suffered some serious losses before, but the thought of losing my girl was fucking with me. I didn't even know the extent of her injuries, but I couldn't wait to step foot in the hospital and find out.

When we finally arrived, Riana and a host of other people from Chelsea's crew sat in the lobby. As soon as Riana came to me to talk, all I wanted more was to see Chelsea. "What room is she in?"

She dropped her head, "There is no room because she's in surgery. They're removing the bullet from her shoulder. They are also running tests to make sure that all the blood loss didn't affect her. Her breathing seemed off, so that's another reason why they decided to take extra precaution."

I slumped into the waiting room chair, shutting my eyes. All I could think was how in a blink of an eye something so traumatic could happen. I knew then I had to make sure to not lose time with her or anyone I loved. But how bad could a shot to a shoulder be? I would later find out.

I must have fallen asleep; A deep voice had awakened me. "Ok, I know Chelsea's parents are on the way but they have given me permission to speak to Riana and Sean." I jumped out my seat, walking over to the doctor and Riana.

"Chelsea's ok, we've done several tests and we know she didn't suffer any brain injury or damage. We are however worried about the amount of blood loss she's experienced. We will be giving her a blood transfusion and... Sean, correct?"

"Yes, Sean Bennett, sir."

"I've spoken to Ms. Riana Jones earlier about her condition, so I am not sure if she informed you exactly where the injury is. We removed a bullet from her shoulder. There's also a graze to the head "

After those words, my heart sank to my stomach. Tears filled my eyes profusely. Which isn't in my nature and I could tell the doctor felt bad to see me like this.

Riana tried to make me feel better, "Sean, she's ok."

Shaking my head, no, "I know she's alive and all, but damn, I love her so much and wish I could have protected her in some way."

The doctor finished talking, "Ms. Jones and Mr. Bennett, I can assure you we will do our best with her. Thankfully, she's stable, but we have sedated her in order to keep her from going into shock. She's very swollen but that should subside soon. Our next step is the blood transfusion since we've finally gotten the blood loss under control. We already have everything we need. Just continue to wait here and by the time we are done, we'll have her placed in a room and her parents should have arrived.

I looked down at my phone noticing it was 2 am. I tried to stay focused but instead decided to look through social media. The media outlets mentioned Chelsea and how her shooting may be because of me and Randall. I knew better than that though.

Then another mentioned it was all about Shooter and how she shouldn't be involved with him. Things went as far as saying #RestInPeace. I put my phone up, I couldn't let my mind go there.

Shooter ran up to me. I hadn't seen him when I got there but it was obvious he was hurting and still in shock. "Sean, I don't know where shit went wrong," Shooter shouted with his head down.

"Do you know who did this?" I asked angrily with my fist balled up.

His tears freely flowed hitting the floor, "You know I ain't the type to talk about shit but yeah it was Pete." My eyes grew in size with anger. Shooter saw that while wrapping his arms around me.

"Sean, I already know he needs to be dealt with and I got something for his ass. Pete and I got into it when I fucked Lexi."

"Damn, you fucked her too?"

"Yeah, and it's a possibility that the baby is mine. We slipped up a few times and didn't use protection, but I didn't know she was fucking Pete too. When I talked to Chelsea a few hours ago, I was getting ready to tell her about everything, but this happened. Pete is behind this because I saw him out the window. Him and two other guys. No one knows this but you. I'mma handle it though."

I couldn't wait to see Pete and his boy Tim. I've had my crazy days in the past and wasn't scared to bust a cap in a niggas ass, but that shit wasn't me anymore. I had grown up and knew I was better than that. But when it comes to Chelsea, I wouldn't mind going there.

I watched her while she slept, she laid there motionless. I didn't know if she could hear me. I just knew she was laying in the hospital bed with pads on her face and a breathing machine connected.

Even laying there, Chelsea was still beautiful but my heart ached for her. I knew she wasn't the type to be in drama, but somehow, she got caught up in something she knew nothing about.

I slept at the hospital for two nights straight and finally went home on the third day. Her vitals were good but for some odd reason, she wasn't waking up. It wasn't like she had brain damage, so what was the problem?

After talking to the doctor and him explaining, I understood.

I stood over her bed on the third day and started talking to her. "Chelsea baby, it's me, Sean. I'm sure you already know that but I wish you would open your eyes and talk to me. I miss holding and kissing you. If you hurry and get better I can give you whatever you want. I swear to God I will.——I was talking to you the other day and I saw tears coming down your face. I don't know if you were able to hear me then, but I felt so helpless. I just want you back." I pulled back to breathe. I started to choke up.

"Oh, and your mom and dad just left to get some food to eat. I'm thinking about going home to get some rest but I will be back tonight. I love you girl."

I made my way down the hospital corridor and sat outside waiting on my driver. Then I received a call that Chelsea woke up. I was back to the 10th floor about to walk through her door but decided against it. I didn't want to barge in, so I took it slow and knocked on the door. I didn't hear her say anything so I knocked again while opening the door.

She turned her head to me and smiled while letting the wetness from her eyes flow. I flew into her arms before I knew it. She sobbed while I hugged and held her. "Thank God you're ok. You had me worried. I was scared that I wasn't gonna have the old you back. Baby, I'm so sorry about everything. I swear I got you and we'll get you right in no time." I went on and on until I heard the sweet tunes come from her mouth.

"Sean, I'm so glad you're here. I need you more than you think. I just need your love. Tell me you still see the beauty in me regardless of my physical appearance."

"Hell yeah you still beautiful. You see what you look like?"

"Yes, I had the nurse give me a mirror."

"Don't ever question your beauty, baby." Chelsea beamed and squeezed me as tight as she could.

The nurse came in advising us of her status and also informed that they would be coming to see if they could get her cleaned up.

Chelsea looked to me with a smile then took her attention back to the nurse, "Excuse me, I did notice the bathroom in there and was wondering if Sean could help me instead?"

The nurse threw her head back, "Yeah, why not? Patients do that all the time. We will get you everything you need but we have to evaluate you first and if everything checks out, it's a go."

An hour later they removed all the IVs from Chelsea and stood her up. I could tell she was weak so I scooped her up, heading into the bathroom. The shower was on and the nurses decided to walk out, yelling they would make sure no one came in.

I had her lean against the handrail, while the water beat against her back. How could I have been so lucky to have this woman in my life? She was more stunning than ever, even in this moment, and I immediately knew, marriage was imminent.

A gauze pad covered her shoulder but other than that, she seemed the same. I used a pink sponge brush to wash her up. I lathered her up, slowly making my way down to her rear. Despite the circumstances, the dire need to touch her lurked within. I cleaned her up and decided to massage her in the process.

"Mmmm," she moaned

My erection shot up, observing her facial expression, listening to the sweet melodies coming from her.

Getting closer to the shower I cupped her breast, rubbing her nipples back and forth. I just wanted to touch her and be near her. Chelsea growled, "join me."

I was bare and joining her in no time flat, caressing her as the water shattered down on us. Breathing into my mouth, she hissed and gasped, "Thank you for taking care of me." Her words were low, but filled with appreciation. Her vulnerability intensified the urge I felt to be with her and in her presence.

We spent the remainder of our time in the shower just holding, caressing and whispering out thanks for each other until the cooling water reminded us that we needed to get clean before getting out. And after we finished, I once again gave thanks that I still get more time with her.

CHAPTER FIFTEEN

CHELSEA

STANDING in my shower with the heated floors up as high as they could go while overlooking the city and billboards was something I couldn't wait to do. Finally, I did just that in my bathroom. I was home after spending a total of nine days in the hospital.

Sean had been so helpful since the hospital stay. When I got home, I noticed he'd finished unpacking all the things that I had moved from Atlanta. I had brand new sheets on my bed, Cam's room was finally up to par and the refrigerator and pantry stood fully stocked. When I say fully stocked, I mean bottled waters for days, cases of Powerade, eggs, milk, bacon, chips, sweets and the list went on.

After taking the most relaxing shower ever and standing under the streaming water for an undetermined amount of time, I decided to get back to work by checking emails and making sure I rescheduled anything that I wouldn't be able to attend until my doctor released me to work. But first, I decided to check my Instagram since it had been a while.

"We miss you, Chelsea."

"Get Well Soon."

"Glad you and Sean are back!"

There were plenty of positive comments but of course, there were some negative too. For instance, *"I bet Lexi shot her ass for being with Sean." "That's what she gets for hanging with thugs like Shooter."* After a while, I decided to post a picture of myself. Why not give them something to talk about?

I had my curly natural hair down and decided not to wear any makeup. I removed the pad off my face since the scar seemed very small. It looked like a scratch at this point and was healing wonderfully.

With my white towel wrapped around me, I snapped for a selfie when a shirtless Sean walked in. "Who you trying to show your ass for?" Sean asked with a grin.

"Shut up, nothing is showing but my collarbone and up." Sean posed for the picture, landing a kiss on my cheek and I snapped away. The picture looked perfect, our background was of the skyscrapers hovering through my bathroom window. Then I captioned, "Still Standing!"

"Babe I know you said you didn't want to be stuck in the house so I made reservations for us at Nobu Malibu. Get dressed." I smiled from ear to ear, hearing those words slip from his mouth. After being held hostage on a hospital bed for over a week, who could blame me? I still had to take it easy, so a night out for a relaxing dinner was a perfect way to ease back into a normal routine.

Sean decided to drive this time instead of using his driver, which was a first. The feel of us riding in his all black, drop-top Mercedes Benz AMG was surreal.

I stared in a daze while Sean drove. I felt wonderful, even as I was feeling some minor residual pain. The smell of the LA streets and watching the sunset gave out a special vibe that was specifically west coast. As we drove through Malibu, the mountain view made me more appreciative of life. Adding Sean to the equation made it feel romantic. But how could I not feel hot and ready when Sean's hands were resting in between my legs?

He had all perfect access since I was sporting a red-plaid button up dress that stopped halfway on my thighs. As he started to rub, I opened my legs wider. Sean pushed the switch, letting the top back up. "Chels, you tryna start something? Keep fucking with me, we gon pull over right now," Sean threatened.

"You know I don't mind. You can make love to me wherever you want," I said teasingly. Not giving him a chance to respond, I unzipped his pants and grabbed his expanding dick. I rubbed it a bit, before putting him in my mouth. He grunted while I reached over to adjust his seat as one hand was on the steering wheel and the other was in my hair. He wanted me to take in all of him and I did just that, letting him hit the very back of my throat.

"Shit baby! Fuck, that feels good," he whispered. I continued as the car came to a sudden stop. It was fairly dark as we were in the cut that overlooked the mountains; straight ahead there was a winding road which let me know we were close to our destination.

I straddled Sean and smirked as he realized my secret, "Damn, no panties, huh?" I looked at him through my sensual glaze while answering his question, "Of course not, I want you to have me whenever you want."

To keep him from saying a word, I shut him up by feasting on his tongue. Our tongues paraded with excitement. His strong hand grasped my face, while his other hand gripped my ass. He slid his finger in me, causing me to go wild. I was already primed up, so I seeped down onto him causing his hard wood to part my inside.

"Fuck, oohh shiiit, baby, I love you," Sean muttered. Hearing his husky baritone vocals drove me crazy causing me to ride him faster. I adjusted my footing on his peanut butter seats. I wanted his sight on my clit and all I was offering. He obviously loved what he saw. "Baby get up and lay against the seat." I followed orders, allowing his mouth to play every game in the book.

I screamed with pleasure, gripping his arms. I could only imagine what pain I inflicted in the process but he didn't seem to mind. He was down there doing all types of damage, murdering that shit. His tongue went into overdrive as he played with my bud while fingering me. I'd been ready to make it rain on him but he wouldn't let up and I had to admit, I didn't want to stop either.

He came back up and crashed inside of me, causing a head-on collision. The sounds of his dick hitting against my wetness turned him on even more and within seconds, he jolted and let out a noise, announcing he was fulfilled. Luckily for me, the minute he went in me after his bomb ass head game, I had already emptied myself on him.

We laid there tired as hell but the breeze from outside made it all bearable. We fixed and cleaned ourselves as best as we could, then we were back on the road. A few minutes later we arrived at Nobu Malibu excited to continue our evening out.

We were greeted and seated in an area overlooking the Pacific Ocean. Since Sean and I decided to stop and have sex, we were a little late for our reservation. I was glad because the view of the moon hitting the water was gorgeous. Sean and I joked around until Riana walked up.

"Yass Chelsea, look at you! You don't even look like someone tried to take you out." I laughed at Ri's joke. We hugged, I was so happy to see her. I knew she had been at the hospital with me but she had a lot to do, leaving Sean and my parents with me.

"What the fuck I look like? Ain't no bullet gon stop me from shining. I always bounce back no matter what, believe that."

"Yeah, like your ass was bouncing back in Sean's car huh?" My mouth dropped open at her comment.

"You always throwing that nigga your pussy, he can wait. —Mhm, I know everything. Sean told us to be here by 7:30

and its 8:40 now. Y'all took so long that we took a walk on the strip."

I rolled my eyes at Ri and ignored her. But then Benji came out and that surprised me. "Speaking of throwing pussy, y'all still fucking?" Ri smiled at my question but then replied, "Yeah, something like that. I've been enjoying him." Benji tried to get a word in but Ri stopped him by kissing him on the lips. I could tell she was actually falling for this guy if she hadn't already.

Nobu Malibu had been a spot we'd hit every now and again. It had the charm to bring any group together and the view from several different seating arrangements was our favorite. After enjoying my tasty meal, I was ready to go sit on the patio.

Sean wrapped his arms around me as we sat on the huge outside sofas. Benji leaned back on the bars overlooking the ocean and somehow, Ri's ass ended up on his groin area. They were actually cute together but I still didn't understand when this truly began.

We laughed, chatted, and gossiped about Shooter and Pete. Sean's emotions seemed to be on full display as he cursed up a storm while threatening to kill Pete if he was the cause of my injury. As much as I didn't want to hear it, I was glad to get more insight into what had happened. I hadn't talked to Shooter but I knew we would eventually have a chat. The conversation reminded me that I had a check in the trunk that needed to be tended too.

A few months have passed since the shooting and I was back to work and my normal schedule. I healed physically and had nothing to feel bad about. Sean and I were in a good place and hadn't heard much from or about Lexi besides what was on social media.

This day, news broke that she delivered her baby, Alexandria Cruz. It was apparent she gave her baby her last name, so it led me to believe no other man claimed the baby.

Sean brought lunch to my house and I decided to give him a friendly reminder of what he promised me. "Hey babe, did you hear Lexi had the baby?" Sean gave me an awkward look with his eyes and shrugged, "Yeah and? I could care less." Then he saw the look in my eyes that I was about to snap and immediately he came over and kissed me until I pulled back.

I put my hands on my hips and rolled the fuck out of my neck while making my demand, "You should care because I want you to get a DNA test ASAP." He sunk into the chair while falling silent to my comment.

"I'll definitely do it, but I gotta figure a plan first. I don't want no misunderstanding about me going to see her."

"Oh, no worries because I will be with you." Sean stared at me and I could tell he was aggravated.

"Babe, I'm sorry but I want to know for sure."

"Or what, you gon leave me?"

I was shocked by his question but then I replied, "I can't say for sure, but after everything we've been through I know I couldn't handle this on top of it; so yeah, I probably would leave."

"I'll take it if that makes you happy. But I know I'm not the father."

Once Lexi was discharged, Sean got his lawyer to set something up for a DNA test and Shooter followed suit. I still couldn't believe Shooter had been fucking that girl too but I guess you never truly know what someone is up to until it comes to light.

Anyhow, Lexi refused the test at first but after a few threats, she agreed.

We were anxiously awaiting the results and two weeks later the guys decided to review the results together. It was weird, you would think its personal but since the world knew, it didn't matter.

We were all at Sean's house having an intimate gathering with our friends. His boys and my girls were all together having a ball. Shooter arrived and this had been my first time seeing him since my incident. Although Sean and Shooter have seen each other a few times since the shooting, we haven't been able to connect.

Once he walked in, he was happy to see me and tears flowed out his eyes. I could see and feel the guilt oozing off of him as he hugged me. He apologized profusely. But I had no anger against him. We talked and hashed everything out. During our conversation, I thanked Shooter again for the check that I had now deposited in my savings. I mentioned the check scenario to Sean, and at first he didn't like the idea of Shooter giving it to me, but then he realized that I was his PR at the time and he understood. Business is business.

Shooter and I joined the rest of the group and of course,

the topic was the shooting and the paternity test results. Sean stood up first saying he was ready because he knew it wasn't his. "Yeah, I hope so, because if the baby is yours Chelsea gon beat your ass and then drag you all through your house and I'mma help her." Ri had everyone at the table laughing.

Sean shot back, "I fuck with you Riana but I can promise you there's gon be some tables moving around in here if you lay a hand on me."

We laughed again, we knew Sean wasn't the type to truly disrespect women, let alone put his hands on one. But I knew he didn't mind putting anyone in their place if it came to it. Regardless if it was via himself or getting someone else to handle it.

"Hell, you keep fucking around, you gon be just like Lexi." Ri didn't like his comment and shot him a bird.

No one knew the inside joke but Ri, Sean, Benji and I, so everyone stayed quiet to his remark.

Changing the subject, "Nah, we gon do it together," Shooter shouted. Sean and Shooter opened the envelopes at the same time as Sean read his to himself, and Shooter did the same. Sean and Shooter sat back down quietly. After careful evaluation, Sean brought his paper to me.

I read it, 'Mr. Sean Michael Bennett you are 100% excluded as the biological father of the minor child, Alexandria Cruz.' I jumped for joy into Sean's arms, straddling him, as he stood there squeezing me. "I told you. I didn't have any reason to lie to you. Now I can clear my name. And thanks for pushing me to get this done." Our friends clapped with excitement. But then we all looked at Shooter. He hadn't said a word.

Sean and Ri walked over towards him and from the looks on their face, this wasn't good. Shooter roared, "The probability of Mr. Roland Jones being the biological father of the minor child, Alexandria Cruz is greater than 99.9999%. Based on our analysis, it is practically proven that Mr. Jones is the biological father of the child tested. He paused before continuing, "ain't this some shit? I'll be damned if I have to be there for that thot! The baby is innocent in this and I'll do what I can, but I refuse to fuck with Lexi."

"Damn bro, how fucking long have you been raw dogging her?" Ri asked.

In unison, we all got quiet. He was still at a loss for words. Sean pulled Shooter away from the group and they walked off talking.

The night for me was positive. But I felt bad for Shooter. I wasn't sure how many times Shooter and Lexi had sex but from what Sean told me, Pete thought the baby could be his. Their beef was because of Lexi, and the bullet was meant for Shooter but unfortunately, I got caught in between.

When everything died down Shooter approached me. "Chelsea, I should have told you about Lexi. I knew you never cared for her, so I stayed quiet."

"Shooter it's ok, I'm not mad at you. Just focus on you and baby girl. How do you feel?"

"Like shit! I don't even know why my dumbass fucked her unprotected. I know better than that!"

Ri interrupted our conversation, "Look on the bright side,

at least you ended up with a baby instead of HIV. It could be worse." Ri had a weird way of making people feel better, but her point was valid.

After the back and forth, we continued talking and drinking. I couldn't help but think how smooth life was flowing in this moment. Now that I knew Sean wasn't the father of Lexi's baby, I felt we could actually go further in our relationship. Truth be told, the thought of marriage with him had been longing, and on my mind for a while.

CHAPTER SIXTEEN

SEAN

IT FELT good to be a free man once I got the results of not being Lexi's baby daddy. The media went crazy, and as usual, Lexi looked like a fool. Shooter wasn't the happiest but I knew he would get over it and be a great dad.

Since the news broke, Chelsea and I been nonstop in the bedroom or where ever we decided to get it in. I was convinced, even a gynecologist hadn't touched as much pussy as I did fucking with Chelsea.

We were in a great place and it was time to make her all mine, forever. We were exclusive but I knew I wanted her to be my wife. The night soon came when I invited all our friends and family.

It was a crisp night in LA, my family made it in town for the festivities of Thanksgiving. This year I decided to host. Chelsea wanted to cook and set the mood for both our families. I already knew her parents and she knew mine but our parents weren't yet acquainted.

I walked into the supersized kitchen and watched Chelsea insert a pan into the oven. It wasn't the pan that piqued my interest, it was the fact that Chelsea only wore a bra and see-through panties. It was a sight to see since I could make out her bare lips smiling at me, my dick sprung up in no time.

As quick as she shut the oven door, I walked up behind her, not giving her a chance to move. Her hands still on the handle, "FREEZE, keep your hands right there. If you move, that'll be your worst mistake."

I felt her twitching as I dragged my fingers, touching her slippery lips while moving her panties to the side. I continued to play with her until I felt her juices running over. She knew I loved the soft feel of her pussy, which is why she always kept it shaved.

A low, husky sounding moan escaped from Chelsea's mouth, "Sean, baby, you know our company will be here in the next hour. I need to get dressed." She whined.

"True, but you don't want me to stop, do you? Your body is crying out something different." She continued moaning, while I turned her around, picking her up and placing her on top of the marble kitchen island.

She stared me down seductively, pushing my hands out the way, only to insert her own finger. She stroked herself while watching me remove my joggers and boxers. I dragged her to the end of the counter as she placed her finger into the warmth of my mouth. I devoured her fingers, leaving no trace of what was once on it. With perfect precision, I rammed all of me inside while grabbing her waist towards me.

Watching her bite down on her bottom lip sent me over the ledge, causing me to grip her tighter and stroke faster. I nipped at her neck and ears, as her walls contracted around my shaft. Her panting grew louder and offbeat, when she wailed, "I—I— can't hold it baby, oohh!"

I pushed both of her legs back and went in deeper. We exploded together, while I collapsed on top of her.

After catching our breaths, I slid myself out, glancing, as she got up and wiped down the counter. "Baby, I'm so nervous for your parents to meet my mom and dad. I know they gon get along. I just..."

I leaned down and kissed her. "Babe, stop worrying, our parents will get along fine. Shooter, on the other hand, he may need to worry," I laughed. "What's the worst thing that can happen besides your dad sucker punching Shooter?"

She sighed then shouted, "Exactly! My dad said he was gon go after Shooter since he feels he is at fault, but we know that's not true."

"I'll talk to your dad and we'll figure it out. Just finish cooking with your fine ass."

Forty-five minutes later, I answered the door letting my parents in. My mom and dad seemed so happy and I could tell they were since they didn't look any older than they did years ago.

My mom looked stunning, favoring Jada Pinkett. Tonight, she wore a pink and green fitted dress, stopping at her knees, with some pink heels. While my dad and I looked just alike, except he stands at 6'7 compared to my 6'5 frame. And his hair was starting to gray but he was doing good since he was now fifty-one years old.

My brothers Benji and Sebastien eventually made it and seconds later, Chelsea's parents walked in. "Hey Mr. and Mrs. Collins," I yelled while embracing them.

"My man Sean," her dad yelled while dapping me up. Mr. Collins had swag that suggested he was that man back in the day. It added to his appeal that he was a major boxer with plenty of wins under his belt. We chopped it up until Chelsea made her way downstairs.

Chelsea paraded with excitement after seeing everyone but was stunned and surprised to also see her grandparents and her two favorite cousins. I figured I would not only invite people that I cared about but wanted the same for her.

By the time everyone made it to the table, we were talking about everything. Then Shooter and Riana walked in causing the whole table to go silent. "Dang, were we the main topic of conversation or something? Y'all looking at us like y'all seen a ghost n shiii—." Riana stopped when she noticed Chelsea's parents.

"Oh, hey!!" Riana yelled while waving at them frantically but Chelsea's dad just watched with anger in his eyes. I knew I wanted a better outcome for the night so I changed the subject by turning on some music. I wanted to create a smooth vibe, so I played a bit of jazz music which blasted through my indoor surround sound speakers. Puzzled looks were beaming my way since everyone at the table knew it wasn't necessarily my style but I ignored it.

"Since y'all done eating, let's all go to the back near the pool. There's some entertainment set up, hope you guys enjoy it." Before finishing my statement, Chelsea looked confused. I grabbed her arms and walked her into the family room to talk.

"What's up, Chelsea?"

"Nothing, just a little frustrated because of my dad. Don't you feel how uncomfortable things got when Shooter came in? Hopefully, a little entertainment will help mellow things out."

I kissed her while pulling her into a tight embrace and gripping a handful of her ass. "Stop worrying girl, I'll take care of it. Let's go outback before I have to put *Long Sean Silver* on you." Chelsea laughed while tugging at my zipper.

We made our way outside to the back of the house, into the patio that was covered with candles. The torches led us out to the pathway that held the guests. I could see the lights glistening in Chelsea's eyes as we strolled along.

Straight ahead of us were a few round tables draped in white linen tops and filled with the people who had dinner with us earlier. The other tables were more people, who she's either been on set with or held some meaning in her life.

She turned and looked at me, with tears in her eyes, "Sean, why are all these people here?"

With a warm smile, I answered, "They're here to celebrate with us, your recovery and our success together.

With everyone seated and staring at us, I spoke up for

everyone to hear me while holding Chelsea's hands and gazing into her eyes.

"Chelsea, you don't even know how much you've added to me. I have grown so much as a man over the years and I owe that to you. You have seen me in some of my most vulnerable times. When I did something that wasn't pleasing, you told me the truth. You never hid anything from me just because of who I was. So many people go along with me because of the money, the fame or what I could do for them. Not you though. You always stood your ground and I thank you for that. My parents taught me how to treat a woman because my dad is a man who embodied that with my mom. But you showed me things that he could never teach. Some things can't be taught and can only be learned through life experiences. I thank you for that. I thank you for loving my imperfections. But don't get it twisted, I love all of you too, the good and the bad. And as much as I love you, I love Camden too. I want to be in his life and wouldn't have it any other way. I always knew I wanted more from you, but like you, I had fears too. Thankfully, we got over that and gave it a try."

"So, what you sayin' Sean? Don't hold back!" Riana, yelled, causing the crowd to break out into laughter.

I got on one knee, as Camden walked up with the ring that we picked out together a week ago. "Chelsea Renee Collins, Will You Marry Mm...?" Not being able to finish because her mouth was on mine so fast, she gasped for air, "YESSSS!!!"

In that very moment, she grabbed Cam and kissed him, crying into his shoulder.

The only thing that stopped Chelsea from crying was the man's voice singing *"Thinking Out Loud,"* from behind her.

My boy Ed Sheeran blessed us with his presence and I was thankful he made it. Although, I was gone have to go after him because Chelsea seemed to be feeling him entirely too much.

Chelsea and I started dancing near the end of Ed's performance. The moment seemed so perfect. I felt that shit in my soul. Every word I said to her resonated in every part of me. Then seeing 8-year-old Cam walking up made me proud. Cam was the mastermind behind what he felt was best for his mom. I really appreciated him for that. I knew that night would be the beginning to something special that I would share with Chelsea and Cam, Forever.

Shooter and I sat in the lobby of TLD Studios waiting on Pete and Tim. We knew they were about finished because our plug was keeping us in the loop.

I grew up in a nice neighborhood and my parents were financially stable. But I followed my cousins' footsteps when I was younger, by hanging with him in his neck of the woods and staying up to no good. My parents were not happy with my actions during those rebellious years.

During that time in the streets, I had my fair share of fistfights and gunplay. Thankfully, I'd changed with age and with the support of my parents and brothers. I was in a different space but if something came up, I was no pussy either. People would underestimate me because they see me as a pretty, light-skinned nigga; but that quickly changed once people started seeing my actions. My temper and the things I'd seen growing up made me who I was.

I got a text to head up and we did just that. Shooter and I busted through the door, Pete was the first to see us. My eyes locked with his, he jumped back immediately with his pupils bucked open, "What the fuck man, you scared the shit outta me bruh?"

I moved into his face shoving him, causing him to fall back. He got up with rage but didn't attempt to hit me. "Pete, I'm gon ask you something and you better not fucking lie to me. Because I swear, I will lay yo ass out right where you stand. Were you in that truck when Chelsea got shot?" Pete trembled in utter silence. I could see the trepidation in his eyes but more than that, I could hear fear behind me.

When I looked to see who was yelling and grunting, I noticed Shooter had Tim hemmed up on the wall with a knife to his neck. *Shiiiit*, I knew Shooter was capable of killing him on the spot, so I understood Tim's panic. But I had to focus on my target.

Luckily, I turned when I did because Pete was drawing up his all black Smith and Wesson Gun. I think he forget who the fuck I was. As soon as I got an eyeful of what he was doing, I slapped that shit out of his hand, causing the gun to make its way across the room.

I was so pissed, I gave him a left hook to his jaw, causing a cracking noise to hum from the bone. The screeching noise that left his mouth was quite frightening. His cheekbones seemed to had been displaced. I couldn't tell if his jaw snapped out a place or if his face just swelled up immediately. Either way, Pete was fucked up and his left eye was barely visible.

I bellowed with rage, "Are you fucking stupid? I tell you what. I'mma take it easy on you. But tell me, were you the one to pull the trigger on my girl?"

He was quiet for a minute but responded while coughing up blood, "I... I was in the truck." He paused gasping for air and trying to keep from choking. He turned his head spitting up blood. "But I ain't the one who pulled it, man. I swear I didn't."

I was a centimeter away from releasing all my fury on him as I yelled, "So who the fuck did it, Pete? I want answers now and if you don't come correct, you will die tonight." He must have thought about it because in a desperate cry he blurted that it was all Tim's idea and they didn't mean to hit Chelsea. The bullets were strictly for Shooter.

Behind me I heard, "Uugghh.... I'm sorrrrr.... Sorry," Tim groaned and my reaction was to kill the voice that had spoken. But looking behind me, I noticed Shooter had gutted the culprit with the knife. It was like a bloodbath. Blood dripped everywhere as Tim slumped over to the floor. My original plan was to kill them if they had anything to do with Chelsea getting shot, but now, I had too much to risk and lose for making a decision like that.

"Shooter, remember the plan. Torture their asses to get as much information as possible. We don't need to kill 'em!"

"Ion give two fucks! If he tried to take me out, that's all I need to know. He gone die tonight," Shooter shouted back.

The old me would have bodied both Tim and Pete, but what was the point? Chelsea survived. But deep down inside, I wanted to make a point that showed them we aren't the ones to mess with.

Pete was so shaken up that he balled up in a corner. I knelt down, interrogating him. "Pete, your boy over there dying all because you were worried about a bitch! A bitch that's been passed around. So, answer this, who—the—fuck—pulled—the—mo—-tha—fuckin'—trigger? You have ten seconds." Pete's nerves were so on edge that he couldn't even utter a sound. He tried to speak but he'd lost his voice.

"Hey Pussy, you don't hear me talking to you? You down to five seconds or I'mma blow your brains out! Four, three, two, —."

"Ai—aight, dayuummm. I had my hand on the trigger but I was shaking and I told Tim to forget it but somehow I accidentally fired."

"You shot Chelsea, hmm...?"

"I'm sorry Sean..." His apology fired me up, so I pulled out my Beretta and pistol-whipped him until he was unrecognizable.

I blacked out until I felt Shooter pulling me off. When I took another look at him, Pete's head was swollen with knots everywhere. I couldn't believe I'd gone off like that. But me being me I still kept talking shit, "Ole Squidward lookin ass."

Pete laid out cold, resting in a pile of his own blood. I knew he wasn't dead so I ain't feel too bad. I turned my attention to Shooter, who was now using a black rag to wipe off the blood on his knife.

"Shooter, I don't wanna kill these niggas but we can't leave em here neither."

"Sean, ain't no one else coming in here tonight. Let me holla at my boy and get him to clean this mess up. I know these niggas ain't gon snitch. I have proof of them shooting Chelsea."

My eyes darted at him, with a raised brow I fussed, "Why the hell you ain't tell me?"

"Bro chill, Sonny the security dude from the arena was able to find it. He said if we need it, we can get it." I brushed it off and listened but I wasn't sure I bought it.

About an hour later, Pete was up and talking crazy, "You niggas fucked up man. Dayuum, I told y'alll sorry, but y'all insist on killing me and Tim, huh?"

"Shut-the-fuck-up, we ain't killing nobody! But if we hear any of this in the streets you could bet your ass that we coming to 4598 Cedar Nest Drive. We gon light your whole house up, starting with you first. I guarantee you won't be breathing after I'm done with you. I ain't with the shits," I threatened.

"You ain't gotta warn his punk ass, Sean."

Shooter turned to Pete, "One word and I'm killing your momma and your daughter. Fuck with me. You know I have several bodies already and killing you and your family won't hurt me none."

I walked over to Tim and noticed he had lost a lot of blood but before saying anything, Shooters boys walked in and cleaned everything up.

I was in a better mind frame after the whole ordeal but when I made it to Chelsea later that night I was a little worried. She had been calling me so I knew I was gonna have to lie and I wasn't trying to start that in our relationship.

CHAPTER SEVENTEEN

CHELSEA

"THIS THE TENTH dress you tried on! Come on and pick out something," Riana nagged. We'd spend an entire day shopping for my perfect wedding dress and I was exhausted. I always dreamed of getting married but no one told me how much work comes with it. After hours of searching, I found it. Thank goodness, I was only two months away from my wedding day.

Ri and I enjoyed dinner at a seafood joint. I felt sick and bothered and ended up in the bathroom for most of the time. "What's wrong with you Chels? At the rate you going, you been done puked your brains out. This your seventh time throwing up today," Ri stated with concern. But I couldn't say another word, I was too busy trying to get my stomach to settle down.

Walking into my condo, Sean was surprisingly there, laying on my reclining chair. He was sleeping so peacefully and I couldn't help but place a kiss on his cheek. The minute my lips touched him, his hands pulled me closer. Our tongues meshed and started weaving, creating a beautiful pattern.

I've felt passion before in prior relationships but this one seemed different. There was a scorching feeling inside of me, something that couldn't be put out, something I never knew existed. Sean showed me a lot in just a few months, but I think the fact that we were friends first played a huge part in it all.

I spoke with my mouth still on his, "Mmmm, hey baby. How was your day?" He didn't reply, but instead lifted my shirt, tugging at my breast. He started sucking on my nipple and gently biting. I moaned and squirmed into his lap. I sat on top of him as he gripped both of my ass cheeks, while still maintaining my boob in his mouth.

We were suddenly interrupted by a knock at the door. Sean went to answer it and in came Shooter. He had a worried look on his face but tried to play it off. "What's up y'all?" He shouted.

I smiled at him, while they talked. I decided to get my MacBook and go on the back porch to work. I wasn't even on it for five minutes before Shooter asked me to come inside.

"What's up, Shooter?" I asked while sitting on the couch. I eyed him and Sean, who were both staring me down with nothing coming out their mouths. "Um hello, what is it?" I shouted to get them talking.

Shooter eventually blurted out, "Look, I did something really stupid about two months ago and I don't regret it but I thought you should know. In case anything goes wrong."

Then Sean started speaking about all the things that happened in a studio with Pete and Tim. I was in so much shock at what they were saying that I didn't know how to process all the information.

I pulled myself up to the edge of my seat and pointed my fingers at both of them, with a nice neck roll.

"So y'all dumbass niggas gon go into a studio, assault them and then threaten to kill them and their families? Are y'all fucking crazy?"

Sean's mouth fell open with no response. I assumed he was taken back by the tone and aggressiveness that flowed fluidly from my mouth. But Shooter had a lot to say, "It wasn't really stupid because we had to check them fuck niggas. Look at what you had to deal with, all because of a nigga who wanted my head. I haven't slept well since that happened to you. Even your dad was ready to put a hit out on my ass.

In case you didn't know, at your engagement party, your dad pulled me to the side to tell me his thoughts and how he was gon take me out. He said the only reason he didn't make that happen was because he knew I would not put you in harm's way and he knew we were good friends."

Sean cut him off quick, "Yeah, I had to jump in their conversation and tell your dad we would handle Pete and Tim. Your dad said he was already on it but I personally wanted to see about them. So, I reassured him that we got it. So, here we are, its handled. I don't think word will get out about it. But if it does, we got that too."

These fools frustrated me because I was not the one to be in any drama. But I knew how to handle negative things in a good fashion, it's what I did the entire time I was Shooter's publicist.

After our talk, I settled into a better mood. At the end of the day, I knew they wanted what was best for me. I also knew my dad was just as crazy as they told me. My dad acquired many accolades from boxing but he was still that street nigga, regardless of how much he claimed to have cleaned it up.

Once Shooter left, Sean gazed at me. It was an expression I had never seen before. He seemed mad, but chill. Sean moved closer and in a soothing confronting voice he shouted, "Chelsea, I've known you for a few years and I thought I knew you well. But the way you talked earlier with anger and disgust, that was different."

His nose touched mine as he kept talking, he leaned in, dropping a kiss on my lip. "But *shiiit*." Another kiss. "That anger." Another kiss. "And rage." Another kiss. "Fuck, that turned me the hell on!" And another kiss.

Listening to him be so surprised, yet slightly forceful at my hood persona turned me the hell on. I whispered into his ear, "Mhm, so what are you sayin? You want me to be more aggressive?"

He pulled back to show me his smile, then he flicked his tongue at my ears, letting it trickle down to my neck. I was ready to finish what we had started before we had company but my stomach wouldn't let me be great.

I quickly pulled out of his embrace and ran into the bathroom. I fell to my knees while gripping the toilet bowl. I was back throwing up and the worst part was the fact I had nothing coming out. Absolutely nothing, just air, and spit. I had purged myself from earlier on in the day.

"Babe you alright, you want me to get you something? Is this the first time you threw up today?" I shook my head no. I couldn't say anything, I was still nauseous and trying to remove something from me that wasn't there.

"Eww, you kissed me and haven't washed your mouth?"

I threw my head back, "Oh my bad."

"I'm just messin, I ain't trippin," Sean said, shaking his head with a grin.

But he continued... "Since I noticed you throwing up for the past two weeks, I got you something."

I heard things shuffling around until Sean was in eyesight. By then I had sat on the toilet and he yelled, "Don't pee, here, take this test." I glared at the pregnancy test with hesitation but listened anyway.

After peeing on the stick, we decided to Netflix and chill instead of waiting on the results. We were both nervous so maybe that would ease our nerves. I wasn't ready to have another kid; My career was taking off and Sean and I were having such a good time being together and growing in our relationship. I feared that having a kid too soon would change that. Plus, Cam and Sean had been doing so much together and I wanted them to have their time to continue bonding.

We had fallen asleep but I woke up first. I made my way back to the bathroom to see what the test results were. We sure were becoming accustomed to taking tests in our new family! Before I had a chance to evaluate it, Sean yelled for me to wait for him. He made it to the bathroom and wrapped his arms around me. I looked at him through the mirror. "Why are we acting like we know I'm pregnant?"

"Because I know for a fact you are. I hope we are," Sean said in desperation.

"You look first and then tell me the results." I continued watching him through the mirror as he lifted the test. A big bright smile ran across his face, "YES! I have officially planted my seed in you. Thank you for removing the IUD, I didn't think you were."

The night of our engagement party, Sean asked me to go to the doctor and remove my birth control. I was hesitant at first, but I did it. I figured I would get pregnant after our wedding but that didn't work out as planned.

Sean was in total bliss with the news of becoming a father and so was I. Unfortunately, that didn't change the fact that I still worried about things going wrong. Sean quickly took the worry away when he swooped me from my feet and took me to the bed, where he buried his face in between my legs.

The next few weeks with Sean consisted of getting final wedding plans together and him nagging me about taking care of myself. He had me and Cam staying at his house daily and the back and forth was starting to wear me out. Thankfully, my morning sickness subsided and I was finally able to keep food down.

"Mom, why don't we move here instead of looking for a new house? Since you are getting married to Sean I think this

place works best and I have a lot of friends in the neighborhood. Oh, and daddy doesn't live too far either." I stared at
Cam, wondering was this Sean's idea.

"I thought about it. I do love this place and it's flawless in
terms of beauty. The best part is it has lots of space for you
and the new baby. I think I will talk to Sean about it."

Cam and I cuddled up on the loveseat in the entertainment room where he loved to spend most of his time. Sean
owned every game system and Cam was the one to benefit
since Sean barely touched them. He owned the old school
PlayStation, Nintendo, Xbox, Wii and of course there was the
newer version to each game as well.

I watched Cam continue his round on Fortnite, listening
to him and his friends throw friendly insults back and forth
on the game. Sean had rearranged the entertainment room to
be accommodating for us. He always had a kitchen down
there but it was never stocked. Since I've been there, he
furnished it and added all my favorite snacks and drinks. He
also made sure to have an extra surveillance video in the
room, to keep me from going upstairs.

I made my way to the second floor, where I found Sean
fixing me and Cam dinner. The smell of Grilled Red
Snapper made my mouth water. I loved seeing a man cook,
and Sean had it going on. He grilled the whole fish with
lemon butter and added shrimp on top. Not to mention the
amazing sides of rice pilaf and green beans, dinner was
looking scrumptious.

"Babe I was thinking... I know you said you want us to
move in together before the wedding and I do love this place...

Annnnd I'm sure you're the one that told Cam to suggest us moving in, so I am agreeing to it."

He placed the pan of rice down and hugged me with so much enthusiasm. I knew he buttered Cam up, but I had to admit, finding another place probably wouldn't live up to the mansion he already had. I had fallen in love with the home over the years anyway. I just never imagined living in it.

I did meet the bougie ass neighbors and they seemed ok. A little too stuck up for my liking but I knew I didn't have to deal with them.

"Cam, hurry up! Come here," he yelled, as his words echoed through the walls. A while later, Cam ran up to him. Sean picked him up into a tight embrace. I could tell their bond had increased. Once he put him down, Cam shouted, "I love you, Sean."

"I love you too, lil man." Tears trickled down my face, I never considered how close they had actually become. I knew they went to a few games together, shopped and hung out and apparently those outings nurtured their growing relationship. I was glad to see things falling in place for the two.

My night ended with some alone time with Sean. He'd fix us a nice bubble bath. He'd been reading every pregnancy magazine and article he could get his hands on, so he made sure the water was lukewarm and not hot. The view from Sean's bathroom of the mountains and winding hills was just as beautiful as my views from my condo, and I loved it! While in the tub, I took a special interest in the mountainside that could be seen through the panoramic floor-to-ceiling windows. The bathroom lit up with candles and the little bit of light shining from outside.

I sat in between his legs in the tub while he rubbed his lips all over me. It felt good to have some big manly hands holding me. "I love you, Chelsea." I squeezed his hands, "I love you too, Daddy." Sean chuckled at my comment. He loved when I talked like that.

"Keep playing, *Long Sean Silver* gon come after ya. I'm trying to let that pussy rest but believe me, I can wake her up," Sean said as a threat. He knew that turned me on and I considered his offer.

"Whatever babe, that may be true but I'm actually enjoying this laid-back moment," I purred while massaging his knee.

After we finished and got dressed, we sat in the backyard in our favorite seat. He purchased a porch swing bed that we grew to love. We found it refreshing to talk and swing in it at night.

Our talk surrounded our future in the house with the baby and Cam. He expressed wanting to take a hiatus away from performing and recording since he was becoming a father. I thought that was cool but I didn't want him gone away from his passion for too long.

I wanted to get back to my career too, I wasn't looking to be a housewife. He didn't like the idea of me working too much but I had to remind him that I didn't want to forget my dreams. My goals were still a priority with or without a baby.

"That's what I admire about you, Chelsea. You make your family a priority, but you still set and go after your goals.

Your drive is out of this world, girl.. That's what makes me want to take care of you. You know those gifts you got a few months back at your old place in Atlanta? Just in case you were wondering, I'm the one that bought you all those pieces from Cartier. Even if we never got together I still wouldn't have regretted getting them for you. You are genuine and should be showered with the best." I was shocked and thanked him over and over. I never asked anyone about it but was glad he confirmed the purchases.

I laid my head on his chest while the seat rocked, taking him all in. I was getting sleepy, when he noticed he picked me up and took me upstairs to our room. We were fast asleep once we hit the bed.

CHAPTER EIGHTEEN

SEAN

RANDALL HIT me up asking to meet him. Since I had no prior commitments, I figured why not. The steam had cooled off since the incident between him and I. I could only hope his ass got his shit together.

I was by myself shooting hoops at a local community center when Randall drove up. He pulled up in his red Maserati. This was one guy that loved to stunt no matter what. Even the attire he wore screamed money. I noticed in our last argument he roared that he was more financially able than me. He couldn't even come close if he tried, but he knew that. My net worth was quite impressive. My investments, savings and business ventures alone killed his entire NBA salary. So, I definitely expected him to come and show off and stroke his own ego.

"Ok, Sean B, I see you with the threes," Randall joked while trying to get the ball.

"You the one playin' for the NBA, I'd hate to beat you. Hell, I'm sure someone out here recording us while we speak."

Randall laughed while starting the game. "Ok, we playin' to twenty, whoever scores that first, wins."

"Aight," I agreed.

We were into the game, sweating our ass off. I work out four days a week but Randall had me tired as hell. That dude's speed and agility was no joke. He impressed me. I never mind giving props when it's due. Damn, he was on fire.

He shot threes back to back. But that didn't stop me one bit. He motivated me, causing me to hit just as many threes as he did, except he didn't miss the last shot, which got him to win the game.

Randall fell to the ground first and I followed. I was glad to see him exhausted because on the court he was a beast. "So, what's up man, what's on your mind?" I asked.

Randall paused as if he was trying to find the right words. "So y'all tying the knot, I hear? I guess, I'm happy for y'all since Cam tells me he is happy with you. He also told me how his friends made jokes about our incident. I felt really fucked about that. So, I'mma apologize, man to man. And thank you for making sure Cam always felt comfortable around you and Chelsea."

Shaking his hand, I grinned, "Man, I understand how it made you feel. It's all good. I was still pissed a while back but shit I'm over it. Like I said before, I love Cam and I know you his dad. I respect that and want you guys to do whatever it is y'all do. Hell, I got you too if needed. There's no reason for us to be beefin' anyway. That's real shit."

I could see the tension easing off of Randall because our talk went from serious to jokes. I was glad we could finally put that bullshit behind us.

"You know I got a charity event coming up? If you not busy, maybe you and Cam can swing through? I think he would love that," Randall shouted.

"Let me know the details and we gon make it happen."

I hopped back into my Porsche to head back home and noticed a text from Chelsea. She sent me a video of me and Randall hooping. That shit was crazy, I hadn't seen anyone around us. Then she sent another text, ***It's nice to see you two getting along. That's why I love you. I look forward to spending the rest of my life with you, Sean Michael Bennett.***

She wasn't the only one sending messages. I had thousands of notifications from Instagram and Snapchat. My life was crazy and I could only imagine what the next month would be like when we got married.

Interrupting my thoughts was a call from Chelsea's dad.

"Hey, Mr. Collins."

"Hey, Sean, I talked to Shooter and he updated me on everything. I'm glad you guys handled it, but I do think Shooter's hot-headed ass could have been more chill. Excuse the language."

I gave a half laugh and continued listening.

"But my real reason for calling is to apologize to you. I can't afford for anything to happen to you. I care about you and obviously my daughter is head over heels for you as well. I hate that you were in that predicament, but regardless of what I said you would have gone after them anyways. From this point on, let's not do anything to jeopardize what we both love more than anything in this world, you hear?"

"Oh, yes sir, I hear you. But you're right, I was gonna go after them anyway. But I think we good now." We talked a bit more before ending our call.

I was glad to be on the same page as Mr. Collins. He'd always been good to me. I met him when I was in Atlanta and Chelsea and I had only known each other for a few months. I picked her up from her parent's house just to hang but he came outside to my car to interrogate me about my intentions with his daughter. I tried to explain that we were friends but he didn't buy that. Over a period of time, Chelsea and I would go to each other's family events and that's how our bond grew. He told me that one day he believed Chelsea and I would get together. I laughed at him, but I'm glad he was right.

I got my driver to drop me off in front of the Gucci store on Rodeo Drive. Something wasn't right. As I walked in, Shooter was sitting on a white seat in a daze. He jumped up when he saw me, "What's up? Took you long enough to get here."

"You know how LA traffic is. I rushed getting here and still haven't had a chance to eat yet."

After Shooter purchased some shades and a shirt, we

walked out and of course, there was a crowd of people yelling our names. Shooter had the idea to walk Rodeo Drive and find somewhere to eat. I could tell he had a lot on his mind, so I agreed.

We walked a couple of blocks as we caught up with each other's lives. I learned that Lexi was being overly dramatic on how they would co-parent. He mentioned she demanded an exclusive relationship with him. When he didn't agree, she gave him an option to pay $15,000 a month for the baby, without going through the court system for child support.

"Sean, is that bitch crazy? Fifteen stacks for a baby that can barely roll over. *Shiiid*, they might as well put me in jail now and throw the whole fucking key away. Fuck that shit." I couldn't even answer him, that was a lot of money. However, Shooter could afford it but Lexi sounded greedy.

"Shooter, I can't tell you how to handle things but there's gotta be a better way. Make sure you get your child consistently and provide for her as well. If Lexi doesn't like it, then get Sebastien on it to establish some order so you could spend physical time with your daughter, while still providing financial support. He's my brother, but make him earn his keep as your lawyer." Shooter agreed to reach out to Sebastien, but still admitted his regret for getting her pregnant. He felt trapped and was regretful for even dealing with her.

After eating at Crustacean, I could tell he felt better. I FaceTimed Chelsea to let her know I was with Shooter. She expressed her concerns about us staying out of trouble. She worried about the incident with Pete and wanted us to promise to leave it alone.

"Chelsea, get off Sean's dick man. He can handle himself, you know?" Shooter joked. But Chelsea didn't find it amusing and before I could intervene, her words were piercing through our souls, like bullets. She fired shot after shot, before closing the casket on us.

"Damn, Sean, I bet you ain't know Chelsea had a mouth huh?" I chortled at his statement. "She fired our ass up and we still burning. Whew, let me go drink some water," Shooter laughed while calling the server over.

I knew Chelsea in and out and from our friendship, I've seen it all. The good, bad and ugly. She carried herself well and was very articulate. Her added street smarts made her well balanced. As classy as she was, she could still hold her ground. Her intentions were good in what she said but I think her overreacting might have been her hormones. She had been moody a lot since becoming pregnant. But I didn't want her stressing, so I decided to call it a day with Shooter.

When I returned home, Chelsea was calm and not dwelling on Shooter's stupid comment. Chelsea had dinner ready and I thanked God for her positive attitude.

"Babe, all this for me?" I asked while looking at the layout she had on the table. There was fried chicken, fried fish, corn on the cob, macaroni and cheese, shrimp and grits and a bottle of Cran-Grape juice, which had become her favorite drink while pregnant.

"Yes, all yours."

"Chels, you are the best thing that's ever happened to me, I swear. But damn, this is a lot of food and I literally just finished eating at Crustacean with Shooter. You cooked seafood and some southern cuisine. You made enough food to feed a prison."

She laughed, "Well, I made all these weird combinations of food because I was craving all of it. I only had a few spoonfuls of each entree. I couldn't help it."

I pecked her juicy lips, still, on her mouth, I mumbled, "I'm thankful baby, thank you."

After wrapping up leftovers from dinner, she had another lukewarm bath ready for us. We enjoyed a night under the stars once we were full and clean. It was refreshing to be off the road and out of the studio. Staying out the spotlight was nice; Chelsea and I didn't have many disturbances from the media once things calmed down with Lexi and I could definitely get used to that.

Tonight, I wanted everything to be about her. In the bed, I opted not to have sex, well kinda. I wanted her to crave me in a different way. Sex life was great but I noticed how happy mental stimulation made her. My words and touch did something to her and that alone got me excited.

I gave her a full body massage and her pussy was no exception. I made her cum back to back with my voice, words, hands, and mouth. By the time I'd finish she was fast asleep.

CHAPTER NINETEEN

CHELSEA

"I DON'T KNOW who the fuck he thinks he is? But he got the right one. I'mma fuck him up if he keeps playin.'" I shouted at Riana, who was grinning while sitting on the bed.

I ran around like a chicken with its head cut off. I yanked all my clothes out the closet, stuffing them into the largest suitcases I could find in Sean's closet. Sean left the house early in the morning, saying he would be with Benji. I didn't mind that at all, but it was now ten at night and he hadn't answered any of my calls or text. That pissed me off, considering I made plans for us this evening.

"Chelsea, you two are getting married in a few days, y'all are living together now, so what the fuck is you trippin' about? Do you think he is out cheating?" Riana asked with an attitude.

Staring at her, batting my eyes, "Um I don't know what I think, but I know he could have at least replied to my text. I also know if you keep talking to me crazy, I'mma knock your head off and I'm not playing. Keep on," I threatened.

"You used to be the classy one in our group. You were reserved and barely cursed but you done turned into a real one. Let me find out Sean rubbing off on you." Riana tried to joke.

After running around like a maniac, I became breathless. I had to sit down and chill. My phone display read 11:02 PM. I walked into the closet and stood there crying. Riana tried to console me. She tried to be a great friend and the voice of reason, but I was too far gone. I still loved and respected her for trying to reel me in..

"Chelsea, can you chill, please? You know my god baby is in there," she motioned while placing her hands on my fairly small stomach. I hugged her then I heard a door slamming shut.

My heart started beating fast as hell, as I shot up from my position, running down three flights of stairs to tell Sean off. Near the last step I looked at him, he gawked at me smiling. "What the fuck you smiling at? You think we gon be doing this? I refuse to be with anyone that can't respect me enough to reply to a simple text message."

I continued fussing while clapping and snapping, only for him to giggle in my face like a damn idiot. I was so furious that I mushed his head back. He acted as if he didn't feel anything by grabbing me closely and dangling a keychain in front of me.

"Get that shit out my face and tell me where the hell you've been? You obviously were too occupied since you couldn't call or text me back." I shouted while swatting the chain out my face.

"Stop complaining. I have been out running errands then I decided to get you this keychain."

I took a good look at it, noticing some fork looking symbol. I still was lost, so I yanked it out his hand and walked off. For some reason, I felt silly and reconsidered if I'd overreacted. When I looked back at the keychain, I noticed more than that, there was a black and silver smart key attached to the weird looking fork symbol.

I got up and walked back to the main entrance area but no one occupied the space. Then I heard a car horn beeping. Walking outside the gigantic double doors, there sat an all-white SUV that was unfamiliar to me. As I got closer, the automatic outside lights came on, giving me an amazing view of this car that seemed brand new.

I noticed the fork symbol again, with the words Levante. Then it all clicked, this was the Maserati symbol. I instantly felt foolish!

I looked inside the car. The black and red leather interior were gorgeous. The oversized in dash seemed bigger than usual. The space in the SUV was immaculate and to top it off, the letter C had been engraved on every headrest.

My heart fluttered with joy when I gazed up. The panoramic sunroof allowed me to observe the beauty outside. I'd expressed to Sean that I planned to get a new car after the baby came. I knew I would need more space. But the main feature I wanted was a panoramic sunroof.

I sat in the driver seat and reclined my chair while smiling with my eyes closed. I was very grateful.

"Yeah, all that shit you talked about me cheating, not respecting you and blah, blah, blah. So, what you think?"

"I think I owe you an apology. I'm sorry for assuming the worst. You're more than I ever dreamed of. You really do listen to my wants." He cocked his head back and continued to listen.

"You make shit happen and I can't ask for more than that. Thank you, baby." We ended up in a deep kissing session until Riana started fussing.

"Look at you, just dumb as hell. Go on and unpack your shit from those suitcases you were about to steal." Sean stopped and gave me a weird look.

"Mhmmm. Don't ask me to help you either. Ain't no one tell you to go assuming and shiii," Riana kept going until I cut her off.

"Girl shhhuuuut uuup," I said with embarrassment.

I later found out that Ri knew what was really happening and the point of her being at the house was to make sure I stayed calm since I was pregnant. She totally failed that mission because I know my blood pressure was through the roof.

Once inside, I noticed Benji sitting at the table with Ri in his lap. I gave them both a look and apparently Ri had more to say, "Ehh Ehh, don't give us that look, like you ain't bustin it open too. I just don't mind being open with it." Then she leaned into Benji, kissing him. They were going at it so much, they might as well had sex right then and there.

Sean grabbed me up from the back, placing soft kisses to my flesh. "Benji, you not the only one that's sliding into something tonight," Sean yelled while smiling like a kid in a candy store.

"Bruh, I ain't startin with you tonight, you already know what's up," Benji motioned while slapping Ri's ass cheek.

I hadn't noticed how thick she'd got until I saw her ass jiggle. I knew someone been putting in some work but I knew it wasn't Santos.

My stomach twisted in knots from fear and anxiety. My wedding day had come and so far things were going great. I was afraid of my dress being too tight but luckily at twelve weeks pregnant, my stomach barely showed.

As I waited to enter the huge Victorian doors of the church, Ri cried while whispering, "Bitch you getting married, who would have thought it would be to Sean. I'm so fucking happy for you. You deserve it." Tears consumed my eyes, but I was so glad to share this moment with her.

I hadn't seen my dad in a while, so seeing him in the lobby before our walk made me giddy. I was such a daddy's girl growing up and that hadn't changed much. My mom smiled so damn hard, it didn't make sense. I wasn't sure if it was joy for me or because of how stunning my dad looked.

My father walked me down the aisle as the man of the hour stood waiting for me to make my way. He was so fucking fine and all I could think was *shit*, he was all mine and we were about to become one for a lifetime.

Sean wore an all-white Givenchy Suit. However, the blazer had an intricate black design which allowed his black undershirt to pop. Halfway through my walk, I noticed his perfect tape up that lined his face and goatee well. Over the past few weeks, he had allowed his low-cut hairstyle to grow enough to create a man bun and this day he rocked the hell out of it. He was a full course meal indeed!

He licked his lips as I approached him but that didn't disguise the fact that he was for real crying in front of everybody. I noticed Benji and Shooter patting his back. It was truly beautiful and heartwarming.

When we made it to him, my dad hugged Sean, handed me over at the appropriate time and took his respective place in the audience next to my mother. Sean pulled me so close that it startled me and the room became full of laughter, as they caught the moment. The chatter was good, it helped lighten the mood for Sean.

The way he glared and gazed at me sent waves through the place, as I heard everyone oohing and awwing. His smile illuminated causing something to ignite in me. I was in tune with him and at that moment, I knew without a doubt that he was for me.

We went through the process of saying our vows to each other, both anxious to get to the moment where we would be official. "You may now kiss——," Sean didn't wait for the man to finish, his tongue slid deep within my mouth. "The Bride."

Finally, the man was able to finish. The guest stood to their feet yelling and cheering.

The ceremony was witnessed by two hundred close friends and family. Even with that number of guests, we managed to keep things private and I had Sean to thank for that. He hired a good wedding planner and an excellent security team. Add to that, the area we reserved on Catalina Island for our wedding and reception wasn't accessible to the public.

Lavender lights radiated the ballroom as Sean and I walked in. Within seconds, smoke came out of nowhere. Once it cleared everyone got a glance of us. We'd changed outfits by then. I sported a gold fitted dress, while Sean rocked all black slacks and a black shirt, with gold suspenders. We tore the dance floor up with our slow dance. Sean was nothing to play with when it came to rhythm and movement. He had all the moves.

Eventually, the DJ sped the music up, playing more upbeat tunes causing everyone to get out their seats and hit the dance floor. The place was lit and the DJ didn't hold back at all. There was music for every person there, from old school to new. Everyone in attendance grooved to the beat.

The reception was beautifully decorated and would be hard to duplicate, considering we made sure to make it authentic and our own. Our King and Queen Chairs were placed near the food. We had a special mix of southern cooking and healthy foods. We tried to cater to our families, who were all about pork chops, fried chicken, fatback, macaroni and cheese, collard greens and the list went on. But we considered our friends as well because they were into healthier food choices. But the way I loved cake, I made sure to add a variety of desserts and of course my favorite, banana pudding.

After dancing with friends and family, Sean and I eventually made it back to each other. "Mrs. Bennett, will you give me this dance?" Sean asked while kissing me. We danced our asses off and everyone tried their best to hang. Then me and Ri's old song came on, and I left Sean to make my way to her.

♪♪ "I'm swaggin, I'm surfin," The crowd swayed left to right. Benji was so amped while making his way through the crowd, poppin bottles. Sebastian, who's usually reserved, had his shirt off and was swaying along with the crowd.. It was a mess on the floor in the best way possible; and most importantly, it was a time to remember.

H-town's, *Knockin' da Boots*, slowed everyone down on the dance floor. Sean stood behind me, as I did a slow wind. I felt *Long Sean Silver* slowly making an appearance. I turned to face him causing him to grip my ass. "Babe, you know all these folks in here looking," I whispered in his ears.

"So... You're my wife now. I'm free to do whatever I please. But what I want is to make love to you, right now," Sean said seductively, gripping my ass even harder. I was horny and ready to bust it open right then and there.

He led me out of the reception hall, into another room, which was fully furnished with some elegant pieces of furniture. Sean shut the door behind us and got naked. My eyes shot open as I stood there. He must've not liked my response, "Babe I made sure I reserved every inch of this place, ain't nobody coming up in here." I rested my head on his firm chest, as he unzipped my dress, causing it to drop. He gripped me up, laying me on a round bed, that felt amazing against my skin.

The passionate kisses he placed around my navel sent fervent waves flowing through me. He explored my body as if it was his first time. Gently, he swept his fingers across my nipple, while he licked and sucked both simultaneously. I moaned and begged for more. He moved lower as his tongue pierced my opening and his hands opened me wider..

"Fuuuck, stop teasing me, pleeease," I cried. My words were useless as he dived head first in between my heat.

He devoured my insides, destroying everything in sight. His head game was good and he mastered it at this point; my head and body were unequivocally tuned to his every movement. I was ready to nut, but he didn't give me the satisfaction. Quickly lifting back up, he took Sean Silver for a ride.

He hovered on top hitting every spot, not missing any chance to fulfill our every need. He continued to drive himself in causing me to move erratically. I tried to back away from the pressure he was applying but he maneuvered me back down towards him. "Don't make me chase you. You been taking that shit." The heat from Sean's breath in my ear created an abundance of wetness in my yoni, which only added to what I was already feeling. I screamed out, "Pleeease baby, oohh, I can't, I can't take it." Tuning me out, he thrust mercilessly. The ride was jagged, pushing me to the edge until we released together.

Our breathing became severely delayed and our sweat dripped profusely. My yoni was officially unresponsive. I was numb and knew my mound had to be swollen. *Long Sean Silver* put her out of commission temporarily and there would be nothing we could do about it.

We laid there for a while with no words until we heard someone crack the door open. "Oh, wow, um, you two couldn't wait for the honeymoon in Bora Bora tomorrow? You do know you'll be there for a whole eight days, right? I'm sure that's more than enough time." My mom kept speaking while covering her eyes.

With embarrassment, I answered anyway, "Mom, oh my God, why didn't you knock first?" At this point, I was dressing myself and Sean had managed to get his boxers on.

"Honey, I did, but you two were so loud. Honestly, I'd rather catch you two than let someone else walk in. And hurry up, people are looking for y'all," my mom whispered while going back out the door.

Sean busted out with laughter and tears. He chuckled so hard that he snorted. "Babe, it's alright. I bet your mom and dad about that life anyway. Hell, we grown."

I disregarded his comment and continued getting dressed while checking my hair in the mirror. Thank goodness I had a fresh sew in. If I wore my natural hair, I would have looked like a chia pet.

When we walked back to the ballroom, everyone was winding down. They looked exhausted. "Dayuum, bitch, you really went and got laid, huh? Y'all been gone for over an hour," Ri alleged with a big smirk. I ignored her while trying to blend in with the rest of the crowd.

The next hour consisted of talking, laughing and saying our last-minute goodbyes to guests. It was such a grand night and I hated for it to end. But I knew I needed to rest and to prepare for our honeymoon.

EPILOGUE

SEPTEMBER 2018

CHELSEA WAS ready to deliver our daughter. She'd been in labor for twelve hours and seemed miserable. I've never seen her in so much pain. The first few hours after her water broke she remained fine but the doctors decided to increase the Pitocin. I didn't know what that drug was for, but I know it did something to her and somehow helped move the labor along. She was now screaming for dear life.

The delivery room consisted of me, Chelsea's mom, my mother, and Riana. Every time Chelsea screamed, Riana screamed. If she cried, Riana followed suit. I ain't never seen nothing like that before. That shit was too funny. But I guess that's what women do. I had to admit, I felt sorry for Chelsea, but that quickly changed when she started fussing at me. She threatened and called me every name in the book. "Baby, why I gotta be all that, huh? You act like you weren't begging for

Sean Silver?" I joked, knowing she wasn't gonna be able to get up but she managed to pop my mouth.

Riana yelled, "Sean Silver? Who the heck is that?" Then Mrs. Collins cut in, "I sure hope it's not what I think they're talking about?"

I laughed and Chelsea went off, "Mom excuse me for my words but shut the hell up Sean, why would you say that in front of everyone? I didn't go after anything. You've been after me remember?—OOOHHH, ok, I think I gotta push, please help me."

The epidural was being administered into her back. I never saw such a big fucking needle before, but I knew there was no way in hell someone would put something like that into my back. I respected Chelsea but watching this made me look at her differently, it made me love her even more for enduring this to bring our child into the world. She stood completely still like a statue while they inserted the needle and I was determined to show her my appreciation forever.

Now it was time to push. She squeezed my hands as she pushed. It was clear she didn't want me near her. She kept shouting as if I was the one physically hurting her. Chelsea worked hard but I couldn't tell who was working harder. I looked to my left and noticed Riana with her legs dangling off the arm of the chair, but she too was yelling. If I wasn't mistaking, she looked like she was pushing too. I was convinced, Riana was crazy as hell.

"Riana, what are you doing?"

She rolled her eyes and fussed, "What does it look like

I'm doing? I'm supporting and showing her how crazy she looks and sounds by imitating her."

The whole room filled with laughter. Even the doctors had to put their head down and chuckle. Man, I had seen it all. I knew I had to warn Benji. I wasn't sure if Riana had it all together but I knew her love for Chelsea was real and I had to give her that.

A few minutes later, my eyes were cloudy. Tightness and anxiety filled my chest. My emotions were of a roller coaster as a head full of dark hair peeked out. The baby's body was almost out and I lost myself. I cried like a baby. The soft side of me came out and I couldn't control it. "It's ok to be emotional Sean B. Men have feelings too, you know?" Dr. Mathis tried to console me.

We dapped each other with our elbows since his hands were occupied. Seconds later, we delivered a healthy nine-pound baby girl. Chelsea and both of our moms were sobbing. Riana was just as emotional, except this time, she stood all in our baby's face. Watching Riana was helpful. I was no longer crying, I was too busy trying not to laugh.

Reality hit when Dr. Mathis told me to cut the umbilical cord. I was nervous but got it done. I had just become a father. So much had happened in just a year that I couldn't believe my growth as a man.

SEVERAL WEEKS LATER

The gigantic scenic backyard was filled with laughter from family and friends. Music blasted through the outside speakers causing many to dance. Smoke covered the cloudless blue sky as Sean continued to grill. Chelsea entertained the guests with Senai Caitlyn Bennett in her arms, who was now seven weeks old.

Both Chelsea and Sean's parents were obsessive over their new grandchild. Senai spent the whole day being passed amongst the four, leaving Chelsea with more free time with her husband.

"Mrs. Bennett, glad you could join me on the grill," Sean cooed, clutching her butt.

"I wouldn't miss a second from being with you, Mr. Bennett."

"Aye Benji, keep an eye on the food for me. I gotta do something right quick," Sean shouted while pulling Chelsea towards the house.

Benji gave him a smirk, while Riana strutted behind him.

Once inside the house, Sean picked Chelsea up, cradling her, with her arms around his neck. "Baby, it's seven weeks, we should wait one more week," Chelsea purred.

He continued into the room anyway. "I'm not gonna dick you down, woman. I'm just gon check on it. Last week the doctor said you were clear to have sex but I wanna see for myself. I need to make sure it's all clear for next week," Sean murmured while opening her legs and sticking a finger between the lips.

He caressed the labia and circled his finger around her vagina.

"Hmm, I think your gynecologist may be right. I don't see any signs of wear and tear. As a matter of fact, you look to be as tight as before. —— Oohh, you feel that? I see and feel something wet coming out. It looks like you're ready! I think I may need to run some more test to make sure I'm right," he whispered.

"Mmm, daddy, please, I don't know about thiiiss," she shuttered with a tingle in her spine.

Sean was butt ass naked with his dick sticking straight out when he grabbed his shaft and rubbed it in between the slits.

"Ssshh, it's ok. I'm just gon stick the tip in and then I'll leave you alone. I'm just testing the waters."

Needless to say, the test results were in, they both climaxed, with no issues. Within forty-five minutes, they were back outside partying.

THE END

FINAL WORDS

I want to thank you for reading Fearless Love. I hope you enjoyed Sean and Chelsea's story as much as I enjoyed penning the words. Book 2: UNJUST LOVE (Benji & Riana Story) is now available.

If you enjoyed the story, please leave a review on Amazon, Goodreads and all other platforms to spread the word.

Thanks again! XOXO

BOOK2: UNJUST LOVE EXCERPT

This book is part 2 in the Bennett Affairs Series. Unjust Love is now available.

BENJI

The sound of splashing water caught my attention as the fellas and I relaxed on the couch in the sitting area next to the fire pit surrounded by water and beautiful women. Sean's pool in his new Calabasas home was modern, but I was still a little leery at being so close to the moving flames.

"Sean, you don't think lighting the pit is a fire hazard?" I questioned.

"Nah, the way this seating area is made, the water won't make its way in here." All of a sudden, he reached for me pushing me towards the pit. The guys laughed as I caught my balance and avoided what could have been a very unfortunate situation.

As I began to my exit, my focus was solely on Riana, who was drinking a Corona and dancing with her best friend Chelsea. The setting sun showcased the beauty she possessed. She favored Alicia Keys when she wore her curly hair out and wild, but today she had a fancy updo. Her long legs shined like golden silk, emphasizing her thick captivating thighs which matched her voluptuous rear. It wasn't that her butt was huge, it was the fact she had such a slim waist and small-sized boobs that made her bottom appear fuller, she was what we called 'slim thick.' Riana is fine as hell and it makes it even better that she is always looking for a good time.

Sean yelled while waving his hands towards my face, "Benji!" I smiled realizing that I never moved from my position, "My bad, I was watching your girl Chelsea with her sexy a—." Sean cut me off as he usually does when someone compliments his crush. "Shut up Benji, we all know you checking for Riana."

The boys and I continued our jokes, but I couldn't shift my focus away from her. "Riana let me holla at you right quick," I yelled at Riana while she rolled her eyes and didn't move.

She treats me this way because I still have some growing up to do. Since she's older than me, slick at the mouth, and still with the shits, I have to be strategic about how I approach her and what I say.

Bruno Mars' Finesse blasted through the speakers, but

the only thing running through my mind was finessing my manhood inside of her.

A few minutes later she appeared. "What Benji? I'm catching up with the girls." I stalled thinking if I should even continue with my proposition. "I'm tryna see if you needed a date to the Film and Music Awards?"

Everyone was quiet while waiting on Riana's response, "Nah, thanks for offering, but Chelsea is attending with me, and with our busy schedules it's too late to change the game plan. Besides Benji, you might not be old enough to ride this ride!" Then she had the nerve to wink at me after saying that! "Really Ri, you only a year and a half older." After her smart ass response, Riana went back to doing whatever, and the fellas went hunting for females.

Once everyone left at the end of the night, I decided to go chill in the hot tub. My mind raced a thousand miles per second thinking about the upcoming football season. Being a star quarterback for the Los Angeles Snakes put a lot of pressure on me, but I had my ways of coping and was always up to the challenge to win.

Riana snuck up behind me, covering my eyes and whispered into my ear, "Stop playing with your dick, boy." I smiled and grabbed the back of her hand, bringing it towards my mouth. I kissed it and to my surprise, she didn't trip by that gesture. "You right on time Ri. Come join me." She moved from behind and stepped in front of me with a confused look on her face. She obliged and took her mesh top off revealing her white two-piece Gucci swimsuit. I stared at the tongue tattoo on her ass cheek that had saliva dripping from it. "Benji put your tongue back in your mouth and stop being thirsty."

"You know what Ri? I would argue with you, but tonight I wanna be on something different. Why you keep playing me?" She made her way into the hot tub and sat directly across from me, set her beer bottle down and completely ignored my question. She stared into my eyes while in deep thought until I made my way closer to her.

ACKNOWLEDGMENTS

I can't acknowledge anyone or anything before **God**! This year has been crazy but the way He set up, it couldn't be no one else to allow me to shine through all these obstacles.

Tamara I know you're sick of me but I don't care. I can't even tell you how much I appreciate your patience and the dedication you put into this project with me. Forget this project, all the suffering you have to deal with when it comes to my many ideas. I can't help it but thanks for hanging on.

Dorothy, Kelly, and Luv I can write several pages but for now, I'll just say thank you!

But the ones that feel and deal with me the most, my immediate family (**C, Chaz & J**). I thank each and every one of you for the continued support and I love you!

I couldn't close this out without thanking the **readers** and **supporters**. Your emails, messages and feedback have been invaluable to me on this journey. I can't thank you enough and thanks for rocking with me.